THEY SOUGHT LOVE

Before she could reply he tightened his arms, so that she was pulled against him in a crushing embrace. His mouth was hard on hers, kissing her fiercely, ruthlessly.

She knew all about his reputation that he was an expert lover, skilled at bringing women under his spell.

Now she found that it was true.

There was devilment in his lips. They knew how to move over a woman's mouth, coaxing a response from her, inciting fires of pleasure that threatened to overwhelm her.

She could feel herself melting, wanting only him, ready to set the world at nothing if only she could be held in his arms. The warmth was spreading through her body, terrifying her with its power to undermine her will.

She would not give in, *she would not –*

THE BARBARA CARTLAND PINK COLLECTION

Titles in this series

THEY SOUGHT LOVE

BARBARA CARTLAND

Barbaracartland.com Ltd

THE BARBARA CARTLAND PINK COLLECTION

Barbara Cartland was the most prolific bestselling author in the history of the world. She was frequently in the Guinness Book of Records for writing more books in a year than any other living author. In fact her most amazing literary feat was when her publishers asked for more Barbara Cartland romances, she doubled her output from 10 books a year to over 20 books a year, when she was 77.

She went on writing continuously at this rate for 20 years and wrote her last book at the age of 97, thus completing 400 books between the ages of 77 and 97.

Her publishers finally could not keep up with this phenomenal output, so at her death she left 160 unpublished manuscripts, something again that no other author has ever achieved.

Now the exciting news is that these 160 original unpublished Barbara Cartland books are ready for publication and they will be published by Barbaracartland.com exclusively on the internet, as the web is the best possible way to reach so many Barbara Cartland readers around the world.

The 160 books will be published monthly and will be numbered in sequence.

The series is called the Pink Collection as a tribute to Barbara Cartland whose favourite colour was pink and it became very much her trademark over the years.

The Barbara Cartland Pink Collection is published only on the internet. Log on to www.barbaracartland.com to find out how you can purchase the books monthly as they are published, and take out a subscription that will ensure that all subsequent editions are delivered to you by mail order to your home.

If you do not have access to a computer you can write for information about the Pink Collection to the following address :

Barbara Cartland.com Ltd.
Camfield Place,
Hatfield,
Hertfordshire AL9 6JE
United Kingdom.

Telephone : +44 (0)1707 642629
Fax : +44 (0)1707 663041

THE LATE DAME BARBARA CARTLAND

Barbara Cartland who sadly died in May 2000 at the age of nearly 99 was the world's most famous romantic novelist who wrote 723 books in her lifetime with worldwide sales of over 1 billion copies and her books were translated into 36 different languages.

As well as romantic novels, she wrote historical biographies, 6 autobiographies, theatrical plays, books of advice on life, love, vitamins and cookery. She also found time to be a political speaker and television and radio personality.

She wrote her first book at the age of 21 and this was called *Jigsaw*. It became an immediate bestseller and sold 100,000 copies in hardback and was translated into 6 different languages. She wrote continuously throughout her life, writing bestsellers for an astonishing 76 years. Her books have always been immensely popular in the United States, where in 1976 her current books were at numbers 1 & 2 in the B. Dalton bestsellers list, a feat never achieved before or since by any author.

Barbara Cartland became a legend in her own lifetime and will be best remembered for her wonderful romantic novels, so loved by her millions of readers throughout the world.

Her books will always be treasured for their moral message, her pure and innocent heroines, her good looking and dashing heroes and above all her belief that the power of love is more important than anything else in everyone's life.

"Those who sincerely seek true love will always be rewarded."

Barbara Cartland

PROLOGUE
PARIS 1865

There was a buzz in the court as the handsome Earl of Torrington entered the witness box. Here, in Paris, he was well known for his free-spending ways and his love of beautiful women.

The more the merrier, as a look at the body of the court would confirm.

There they all sat, his current mistress, his past mistress and two hopeful women who were probably earmarked for the future.

They were splendid, buxom and magnificently dressed. Two of them were married to government ministers.

The accused was a huge, powerful man, sullen looking, in his thirties, with a slack mouth and a bitter look in his eyes. His name was Pierre Vallon.

He had stolen jewels from his mistress. Unfortunately for him the jewels had been given to her by Lord Torrington, another of her admirers.

When the jewels had been offered to his Lordship by a dealer, he recognised them and laid a trap for the thief.

Without betraying his inner rage, he had shown interest and said that he would also like to purchase any other jewels that the man could bring him.

Then he had lain in wait. The police were present as well, but it was Lord Torrington who had tackled the thief personally. Vallon had responded by drawing a knife and for a while the two men had fought.

In the end Lord Torrington had prevailed. Although not as large as his opponent, he was fitter after spending many mornings in the gymnasium, practising martial arts.

It was also whispered that the exercise he received in a multitude of different beds had left his body fine-tuned and powerful.

The newspapers made a huge fuss, praising Lord Torrington for his courage and his devotion to justice.

But the real reason, as everyone knew, was his jealous rage over the man who had dared to sleep with a woman the Earl regarded as his private property.

A hum of approval went round the court as the onlookers considered the Earl's appearance.

Thirty, tall, broad shouldered, handsome, with dark looks and brooding eyes, he was a sight to draw any woman's admiration.

At last the verdict of guilty was pronounced and Vallon was sentenced to ten years in prison. He had stood impassive until then, but now he turned his venom on the man he blamed for his imprisonment.

"Curse you!" he screamed. *"Curse you!"*

The next moment he had leapt out of the dock and hurled himself at the Earl, his hands outstretched to his throat.

It took three men to pull him off and even when they succeeded Vallon did not give up. He was still howling curses as they hauled him away.

"I will come back," he shrieked. "You haven't heard

the last of me. I'll be a step behind you every moment, and one day I'll make you regret what you've done. I'll get my revenge and it will break your heart."

"Nonsense!" came a female voice. "He has no heart. Everyone knows that."

There was laughter as Vallon was dragged from the court. Lord Torrington felt his throat and gave a conspiratorial grin at the lady who had spoken.

"How well you know me, my dear," he called.

"But of course! If you had a heart you would not be Lord Torrington and how disappointing that would be."

More laughter and the merry party left the court. Nobody gave another thought to Pierre Vallon.

CHAPTER ONE
ENGLAND 1867

"I think you are the most beautiful woman in the world, the most enchanting, the most bewitching – "

"Please!" Celina Storton tried to silence her admirer, although she found it hard not to laugh.

The Marquis of Delaine was a well meaning young man, and there was no doubting his sincerity, but nature had created him the wrong shape for passionate declarations.

He was large, wide and heavy. The most expensive clothes would never make him elegant, any more than the best tutors could made him clever.

"Don't say any more," Celina begged. "We should return to the ballroom, lest people notice our absence and talk."

"But I haven't finished," he said determinedly. "And I want them to talk, let them all speak of our engagement."

"There is no engagement – "

"But there will be if you will allow me say what I am trying to say."

"Very well," Celina agreed, resigned but also sorry for him. Of all her suitors he was the richest and the most high-born. It was such a pity that she could not fall in love with him.

Taking a deep breath, the Marquis sank down on one knee. He was evidently determined to make his proposal properly, and even cast a surreptitious look at a scrap of paper hastily pulled from his pocket.

"My dear Miss Storton, I offer you my hand and my heart. Only be mine and you will be the Mistress of Delaine Castle – "

Behind him the door of the little anteroom opened and Lady Keller, hostess of the ball they were attending, looked in. But as soon as she saw what was happening she retreated hastily.

Celina sighed and braced herself to hear out the rest of the saga. Finally the Marquis took out a diamond ring with a huge stone and tried to put it on her finger, but she hastily clenched her hand.

"Forgive me, my Lord, but I am unable to accept your flattering offer."

"You cannot mean that."

"But I do. I am not sufficiently highly born to be the wife of a Marquis. My father was merely the younger son of a baronet – "

"A fig for these quibbles!" he cried dramatically. "True love conquers all, and my Mama is quite reconciled – er, that is, she is overjoyed at my choice of bride."

Celina, who had met the Marquis's redoubtable mother, choked back her laughter and replied in a quivering voice,

"I am honoured by her Ladyship's approval, sir, but it cannot change my decision."

"There is another man!" he screamed at once. "But he does not love you as I do."

"There is *no* other man," she said firmly. "But I am unable to return your feelings. And now, sir, I insist on returning to the ballroom, as I do not wish to be the object of gossip."

But that was a faint hope she realised as she escaped him. Lady Keller was a kind woman and a good friend, but she was incapable of keeping what she had seen to herself.

Her return caused a stir, for of all the young ladies who danced and flirted their way through the London season, she was the most in demand.

This caused much heart burning amongst her rivals, for she was certainly not the best looking, nor the most highly born, nor the wealthiest, nor the youngest.

By what right, they asked, did Miss Celina Storton deserve a Marquis at her feet, eager to shower his wealth on her, despite her own comparative lack of fortune? For she was twenty-five years old, well past her best, worth a mere twenty thousand pounds and should call herself lucky to ensnare even a baronet.

She was not precisely plain, but her features lacked that certain something that was real beauty. Nature had given her intelligence and her face reflected it. Her chin was neat and firm, her nose dainty and decided.

Her eyes were certainly lovely, being large and deep blue, but it was what lay hidden in the depths of those eyes that enchanted her admirers.

A sharp wit and a roguish charm lurked there, making men seek her company while other lovelier damsels remained wall-flowers.

In addition she carried herself with an 'air' that had nothing to do with looks.

Tonight she was at her best with her shiny fair hair arranged becomingly in curls. Her dress was blue satin with flounces of lace, tiny roses at the waist and pearls adorning her neck and ears.

And there were many men who admired or even

adored her, but she had eyes for none of them. Lord Delaine had said that there must be another man and she had denied it, but only because this was a subject she could not bear to speak about.

She would die rather than admit that she had given her love to a man who did not return it.

With a sinking heart she saw Lady Keller advancing towards her.

"Well!" her hostess exclaimed excitedly. "What did I see? My dear, I am so sorry for bursting in. I do hope I didn't interrupt at an inopportune moment."

"Not at all," Celina said.

"He did propose, didn't he?"

"He did propose."

"Oh, how wonderful! You will be a Marchioness and have all the money in the world. He will load you down with diamonds and rubies and you will constantly attend Court."

As Lady Keller had three unmarried daughters this was really very generous of her, but Celina was unable to join in her ecstasies.

"I rejected him," she admitted flatly.

Lady Keller greeted this incredible news with a little scream.

"You did what? My dear, what are you thinking of? Nobody rejects a Marquis."

"I do not love him."

"What has that to do with it?"

"A good deal. When I marry it must be to a man that I am in love with."

"And are you in love with any man?"

"No," Celina said untruthfully.

"Then, marry Delaine now and if you fall in love later,

well – these things arrange themselves."

"You mean – take lovers?" Celina asked, horrified.

"Well, of course you must do your duty first. I believe two sons is the bare minimum that is required before a wife may please herself, but – "

"Stop, stop!" Celina cried, aghast.

Of course she had known that many women in high Society amused themselves with affairs of the heart, and their husbands pretended not to notice, because they too were enjoying their extramarital interests.

Nor was it considered beyond the pale if she passed off a love child as her husband's progeny, always assuming that she had first performed her duty in the matter of an heir.

Many a husband had accepted an infant that looked nothing like him in return for his wife's silence about his own activities outside the marriage bed.

But this was not the kind of marriage Celina wanted.

She would wed the man she loved or nobody. And they would love each other so deeply that neither would look at anybody else.

If only –

"My dear," Lady Keller persisted, "I am only being realistic. You have been the success of the Season. No young lady could ask for more. But the time is coming when you must choose a husband. Every eligible young gentleman in London has laid himself at your feet – metaphorically speaking, of course – "

"Not always metaphorically," Celina could not resist parrying mischievously.

"Yes, I have heard those stories. They say young Viscount Buckley had difficulty getting to his feet, being so fat!"

"I begged him not to kneel," Celina pointed out. "But he insisted."

"He was so madly in love with you. And still he didn't win your hand."

"Well, I cannot marry a man simply because he will not listen to wise advice and is too fat to stand up," Celina replied, unarguably.

"Never mind him. You cannot seriously mean to reject poor Delaine."

"I am afraid I do."

"Then who do you mean to accept?"

"None of them," Celina replied with a little sigh. "I know it is very ungrateful of me when you were kind enough to invite me to stay with you in London and sponsor me for the Season."

"Well, one of your friends had to do something. You should have been a *debutante* years ago, and you would have done if your Uncle James had not been such a selfish stick-in-the-mud. What was he thinking about to allow so much time to pass?"

"It is partly my fault, madam. I was happy at home and a Season never seemed so important to me."

"How you expected to find a husband without one, I cannot imagine. How many eligible men are there in your corner of Surrey? Pretty few. There is Lord Torrington, of course, but he spends most of his life abroad, and he is so selfish that he will probably never marry."

"Lord Torrington isn't selfish," Celina responded indignantly. "He just hasn't found the right woman."

"When a man with all his advantages reaches the age of thirty and unwed, take it from me, he isn't looking very hard," Lady Keller said caustically. "Anyway, you need more choice than that, and I thought when I invited you to spend the Season here, that something momentous would come of it."

"I hoped so too," Celina breathed. "I wanted to meet a man I could fall in love with."

"Romantic dreams are dangerous, Celina. Life is not like that. I fear you will always be doomed to disappointment."

"You may be right, madam. Perhaps I should return to my home since I do not deserve your kindness any longer."

Lady Keller begged her to stay for as long as she liked, but Celina was resolute in her determination to leave tomorrow.

At last the ball was over and Keller House stood dark and echoing after the gaiety.

In her bedroom Celina removed her magnificent gown, donned her lace nightdress and then sat quietly at the dressing table while her maid brushed her hair.

"We will be leaving tomorrow, Sadie," she said.

"Oh, miss, what a pity!"

"Not really. It will be nice to go home and see Uncle James again."

'Home' was a fine country manor owned by Sir James Storton, Baronet, who had raised Celina since her parents died ten years ago.

Uncle James was a kindly but eccentric man who spent his days in 'scientific' pursuits. He knew all there was to be known about plants, birds and insects, but nothing at all about the proper upbringing for a young girl.

He oversaw her education, rejecting many governesses as insufficiently academic and finally taking over most of her lessons himself.

Otherwise he left her to her own devices, with the result that she was far more intelligent than young ladies were supposed to be, and lived a social life of almost complete freedom.

Despite his eccentricity Uncle James was popular with his neighbours and received invitations everywhere, even to the home of the Earl of Torrington.

When the Earl had died ten years ago his widow had continued to invite her old friend, half hoping that he would be a good influence on her wayward son, Robin, who had inherited his father's title.

It was a vain hope. The young Earl was wilful, headstrong and self-indulgent. He spent money at a vast rate – he gambled and had adventures with disreputable women. His virtuous mother was said to be in despair.

But to the fifteen year old Celina, the young Lord Torrington was a God. One look at his dark brooding eyes and the locks of hair falling over his brow was enough to send her into a dream of delight.

The stories of his wild exploits made her gasp with horror even while they filled her with excitement.

She had many chances to enjoy his company. Robin was determined not to be pressured into marriage, so her very youth was an advantage to him, as even his Mama did not expect him to court a girl of fifteen.

He regarded Celina as a sister who would run his errands, provide him with an alibi when he did not care to explain his many absences in too much detail, and ask only for praise in return.

In this he was mostly right. Celina could survive on a kind word or a smile from him. But secretly she lived in a blissful fantasy world in which he would suddenly realise that he had fallen madly in love with her.

Looking back, she could not have said when her childish hero worship had turned to love.

She only knew that one day the mere sound of his name could make her heart beat faster, and if he walked into the room she was almost overwhelmed by the force of her feelings.

She dreamed of the day he would ask her to marry him, but, side by side with her romantic dreams, lurked a vein of realism that forced her to face the truth.

'I really have no chance,' she would tell her mirror. 'Look at me, how plain I am. And his life is filled with beautiful girls with accomplishments to enchant him. My chief asset is that I can ride as well as any man. He told me I could. He said it made me just the girl that a man needed as a sister."

She had been eighteen when he had made that devastating pronouncement.

He had recently returned from Paris where he had lived a life of 'disgraceful indulgence' according to his mother, although she had not elaborated further to Celina's virginal ears.

Her attempts to glean more details from Robin himself had been unsuccessful.

"Not you as well," he had groaned, half laughing. "You are as bad as my mother."

That had silenced her.

"Thank Heavens I can come home and talk to you like a sister," he said. "You are the only person I can confide in. You don't judge me and I can tell you how I feel."

"I want you to tell me everything about how you feel," she had said breathlessly.

"I have an overpowering need for freedom. At the least sign of restriction I feel I will go mad. My mother can never understand that."

"I think she is only worried in case you come to some harm," Celina said carefully. "She fears that the – ladies with whom you associate do not love you for yourself alone."

"Heavens I hope not! What a bore that would be! The 'ladies I associate with', as you so cheekily put it, are interested in brief liaisons from which they emerge rather richer than when they started. That suits them and it suits me."

"But don't you mind that they are simply taking advantage of you?" she asked, trying not to sound as shocked and dismayed as she felt.

"Of course not. Since I am taking advantage of them, I prefer it. No obligations on either side."

"I suppose that arrangement could be very convenient," she mused, trying to sound worldly wise.

"I'll say it's convenient. We both know what we're in it for, it's a fair bargain on both sides and I don't have to put up with tears and reproaches when it's over. Lord, how I hate weeping women!"

"Perhaps you give them reasons to weep?" she suggested lightly.

"I pay my debts in diamonds and pearls. I am damned if I am paying them in pretty speeches as well!"

He checked himself suddenly.

"I suppose I should not be talking like this to a well bred young lady," he admitted, with a touch of conscience. "The point is, I cannot really think of you as a young lady."

"I know. You just see me as your sister."

"Or even my brother – you are so sensible and clever. Anyway, I never feel I have to watch my tongue with you and that is such a relief."

"You know you can always talk to me," she murmured happily.

It was not until later, lying in bed at night, that she realised all the dismaying implications of his words. To be his sister – much less his brother – was not what she wanted at all. She wanted him to look at her with shining eyes and worship at her feet.

But, for the moment, she felt a kind of happiness to know that she was the only person that he could talk to freely.

She was guiltily aware that she had done Uncle James an injustice. Lady Keller had blamed him for not bringing his niece to London for a Season six years earlier.

But, in fact, Uncle James had offered to 'do something about it' and she had declined, after ascertaining that Robin would not be going to London. He planned to spend the time on his estate. Once she knew that, nothing could have drawn her away.

The following year the same thing happened. Robin arrived in the country, Uncle James conscientiously offered her a Season and once more she declined.

After that Uncle James had given up for which he could hardly be blamed.

As he grew older and even more eccentric, Celina gradually took over the management of his estate. It was something she did well and gave her great pleasure and satisfaction.

Gradually she settled into a life that consisted of work, riding, local parties and the occasional visit from Robin.

Much of his time was spent abroad, but now and then he would return to oversee affairs at Torrington Castle, spend time with his Steward and host a party for his neighbours.

At these parties she would dance with him. For days beforehand she would look forward to the time when they would waltz together, and she would be held in his arms, however formally.

For just a few precious moments she would be close to him, feeling his body moving against hers, dreaming that they were lovers.

She harboured vivid memories of the last occasion.

There had been a new face in the neighbourhood, Lady Violet Manyard – pretty, rich, accomplished, highly connected and the perfect finished article for an Earl who needed a wife.

This would be her first meeting with Lord Torrington and everyone was holding their breath to see if she could succeed where everyone else had failed.

Robin's mother was especially eager.

Celina tried hard to think the right thoughts. If this girl would be a good wife for Robin, she would try to be glad for him.

But from the first moment she realised that Lady Violet was not a pleasant young woman. She was proud and haughty and among her doubtless virtues generosity found no place.

Her first glance at Celina made it clear that she knew who she was and regarded her with contempt. Her eyes raked her up and down, silently saying, '*old maid*', and she made a little contemptuous sound before turning away.

Robin performed his duty for the first half of the evening, dancing with Celina, Lady Violet and various other local damsels who still had not given up hope. Then Lady Violet again, apparently oblivious to her simpering.

His next dance was with Celina, but this time he cut it short, drawing her into the library, saying,

"That's enough dancing. Thank goodness I don't have to do the pretty with you. Talk to me. Make me laugh."

"For shame," she replied, teasing him. "There are so many local maidens out there waiting for you to flirt with them."

"I am bored with flirting. It's too tame for me." He poured himself a drink and sprawled in a chair. "In fact I am bored with everything. There are times when the whole world seems to have lost its savour."

He became aware of something strange in the way Celina was looking at him.

"What's the matter?"

"Your manners are the matter," she scolded him with mock severity. "Are you not going to offer me some wine?"

"Good Heavens, you don't have to wait for me to ask, do you? There's the decanter."

"I'll take that as an invitation," she responded wryly, filling a glass for herself.

He grinned.

"You don't need an invitation. You have been at home here for years."

'Like that footstool beneath your feet,' she thought, trying not to feel bitter.

The next moment she said, in an apparently casual voice,

"By the way, what do you think of Lady Violet?"

He groaned. "Is my Mama parading her for my benefit? I feared as much."

"She is a most excellent young lady, accomplished and virtuous."

"Heavens above!"

"It is time you were thinking of marrying and setting up your nursery. I have decided that she is exactly the wife for you."

She was guiltily aware that she was ruining that lady's chances with every word. Nothing could more surely alienate Robin than to find that the neighbourhood had virtually married them off.

'I am not being very nice,' she thought with a touch of shame. 'In fact, I am *wicked*.'

But she had the reward that often comes to the wicked, when he took her back into the ballroom and danced every remaining dance with her, pointedly ignoring all other females.

Lady Violet departed early with her Mama, threw a screeching tantrum and married an elderly Viscount the following year.

But that night had been a turning point for Celina.

As she lay in bed that night she knew that she could no longer hold herself in readiness for a man who would never love her.

Lady Keller happened to be in the neighbourhood visiting her elderly mother. It was a simple matter to invite her to a little soirée, and coax from her an invitation to spend the next Season in London.

"You are going to enjoy a wonderful Season," her Ladyship declared.

'Yes I am,' Celia promised herself. 'I am going to meet eligible gentlemen and find myself a splendid husband. I am going to break Robin's spell over me and then – and then he will regret losing me, but it will be too late."

It all happened just as she had planned. She had taken London by storm and received four proposals.

But it was all for nothing. Her hope of rooting Robin out of her heart had been a false one. His hold was as firm as it had ever been.

And now here she was, on her way home, as much in love as ever with a man who cared nothing for her and facing a future without hope.

CHAPTER TWO

The Earl of Torrington leaned back against the carved pillar of the four poster bed, and took a long luxurious look at the beautiful woman reclining against the pillows.

She knew he was watching her and stretched out languorously, displaying her magnificent body in its scanty, transparent nightdress.

Through the flimsy material he could see her generous breasts, tiny waist and magnificent haunches.

She boasted black hair and dark eyes whose depths suggested fathomless passion. He had experienced that passion, for Colette knew how to give full value, as he did himself. The ruby necklace that she was holding up to the light was certainly proof enough.

"Robin *mon cher*," she cooed, "you are always so generous to me."

"My generosity is matched by your own," he grinned. "I declare I am quite worn out."

She, in her turn, leaned back to regard his handsome form which, like hers, was barely clad in a night shirt.

He was a well-built man, with long legs and muscular thighs. His shoulders were broad, a fact that his elegant day clothes often disguised, but which were now very evident.

He looked what he was, a healthy, lustful animal, with generous appetites that he was used to satisfying completely and without delay. Since he had inherited his title everything he desired had fallen into his lap.

These days that often included a different woman every night, although Colette had been occupying him a good deal recently.

The fact that he was rich was well known amongst the French.

Almost every woman he had slept with boasted beautiful jewels given to her by the Earl and which were the envy of all her friends.

He attended the theatre nearly every night and sat with one beauty by his side while his eyes roved over the other beauties in the audience. He was rumoured to be taking his pick, for it was well known that any woman he desired would simply fall into his arms.

None of them lasted long, because wherever he went there was always another woman to be excited by his appearance and even more excited by the stories that were told about him.

He was not only handsome, but there was something in the way he talked and the expression in his eyes which made almost every woman he met fall in love with him.

Colette, reclining amid the luxurious pillows, was as certain of his passion as of her own. To her mind they were the ideal couple and with a little cleverness she could coax a proposal from him.

"Why are you looking at me like that?" he asked, grinning.

She hastily adjusted her expression in case her ambition had been reflected in it too accurately.

"I was just admiring your looks, as I always do," she murmured. "You are what they call 'a fine figure of a man'."

"And if any woman has reason to know that, it's you," he observed with a laugh.

"You must let me come to the gymnasium with you one day and watch you exercise."

"Sorry. No females allowed!"

"Oh, you men! I want to know how you came to be so strong. How I love to feel your strength when you hold me in your arms!"

She gave a sudden laugh.

"Do you remember that man, the one who tried to steal diamonds from you?"

"You mean Vallon? That was two years ago."

"I have often wondered who was the lucky lady who finally received those diamonds, after you had recovered them? I know it wasn't me."

"Naturally not. In those days we did not know each other nearly as well as we do now."

"Oh, yes, we know each other very well indeed, don't we?" she purred. "I venture to think nobody has ever known you as well as I do."

Diplomatically, he did not answer this parry. He allowed every woman to think she knew him better than anyone else.

The truth was that they knew only one aspect of him. Beneath his bonhomie he guarded his privacy very carefully, giving just as much of himself as suited him.

"I think Vallon must have been most surprised to discover your strength," Colette mused. "They say you subdued him with one movement."

"Why should we think about him?" the Earl asked with a shrug.

"Perhaps you *should* think about him, after the way he vowed revenge."

"He may have vowed revenge, but he will be hard pressed to carry it out. His prison sentence still has some years to run. Forget him. We have to decide how to spend the rest of the evening."

Colette gave a throaty laugh, calculated to entice him and followed it up with a little wiggle of her hips.

"Have you any suggestions?" she asked.

"Well – "

He stopped, alerted by a sound from below.

"Great Heavens! What is that?"

The sound continued to rise. With dismay, Colette recognised a woman's voice.

"It's nothing," she said hastily, trying to wind her arms around him. "Make love to me."

"Just a moment."

Skilfully evading her arms, he rose from the bed, pulled on a rich brocade dressing gown and walked to the door.

"Don't go," Colette pleaded huskily. "Stay with me."

To underline her point she stretched out on the bed, contriving to reveal even more of herself.

"You look glorious," Robin said appreciatively.

"Then come here to me!"

"I will only be a moment. Stay just like that."

Then he was gone, leaving Colette wanting to scream and throw something at the closed door.

From below Robin could hear the sound of increasing commotion. A woman was shrieking,

"I will not allow you put me off! I demand to see him. *Let me pass.*"

He grinned. Trust Monique to make her presence felt.

Hurriedly he descended the stairs, calling to his harassed footman,

"It's all right, Francois, this is a friend of mine."

Francois cast him a look of reproach, for it was well known that no lady was allowed to intrude on his Lordship whilst he entertaining another female. But Robin merely signalled for the footman to move aside, then advanced, open-armed, on Monique.

From her dress and jewellery she was clearly a high-born lady. From her wedding ring, she was married. And from her flashing eyes she was in a temper.

She turned on him like a whirlwind, with a torrent of jealous reproaches.

"She is here isn't she? I know she is. Faithless one! How could you so deceive – ?"

The words were cut off by his mouth, pressed crushingly on hers. His arms wound around her tightly, leaving her with just enough breath to kiss him back.

When she had almost fainted in his arms, he loosened his grip slightly.

"Now, be good," he commanded. "Not another word."

For a moment she was incapable of anything except a long, blissful sigh. But then her head stopped spinning long enough for her to cry –

"*Deceiver*!"

His response was to kiss her again. For a few moments she fought him, but again her arms fell slack.

"That's better," he said approvingly. "There is nothing to make a fuss about, Monique."

"You have another woman."

"I have a dozen."

"You are unfaithful to me."

"No, I am always faithful – when I am with you."

"But when you are not with me – "

"Then I am being faithful to someone else. Why worry about it."

"You think every woman in Paris is part of your harem!"

"Monique, you are entrancing."

"So are you. Let's go upstairs."

"I don't think that is a very good – "

His words were cut off by a shriek from Monique, who was staring and pointing over his shoulder. Following her gaze, he saw Colette descending like an avenging fury.

"Oh, no," he groaned. "Ah, well, there's only one thing for it.

"Ladies, ladies," he cried, just managing to hold them apart, "there is no need for this. Come now, let us all be friends. There is love to spare for everyone."

Still holding them, he turned and began to climb the stairs. They went with him, reluctantly at first, then with resignation and then with growing excitement.

As he vanished into his bedroom and closed the door, they were all over him.

In the hall below Francois regarded this retreat with awe. To think people said the English were cold!

*

It took a few days for Celina to settle into her home again. Uncle James was pleased to see her and did not seem too distressed that she had not secured a husband. She guessed that he secretly did not want her to leave.

Some of her neighbours came calling, to welcome her home and ask curious questions about London. And from the Dowager Lady Torrington came a note,

'*My dear Celina,*

How nice to have you home. I would have called on you before, but I am feeling a little unwell. Do come to see me and tell me all your news.

Letitia Torrington'

Celina journeyed straight to Torrington Castle, driving the pony and trap herself.

The Dowager received her lying down on the sofa.

"I am so sorry you are not well, ma'am," Celina said, receiving the older woman's embrace and hugging her back.

"All the better for seeing you, my dear. How lovely to have you home again."

"I want to hear all your news," Celina asked, trying to sound casual. "Do you hear anything from Paris?"

"You mean from that infuriating son of mine? Well, I hope we may see him here fairly soon?"

"Really? Does Paris begin to bore him?"

"I think he is beginning to understand that rank brings its obligations," said the Dowager, choosing her words carefully. "He is now thirty and it is time he did his duty."

"But people have been saying that ever since he inherited the title," Celina remarked, laughing. "He has never yet taken any notice."

"Well, things may be changing," the Dowager replied vaguely. "But now, let's talk about you. I expected to see you flaunting a huge diamond ring after your Season in London."

"Why, whatever can you mean, ma'am?" Celina enquired with mischievous innocence.

"We hear rumours, even here. I gather you took the social world by storm and received any number of proposals."

"But did you hear of my accepting any of them, ma'am?"

"I heard of several that you would have been wise to accept."

"All at once? Would that not cause a good deal of talk?"

The Dowager laughed heartily.

"Wicked girl," she chided. "Now, seriously, tell me if you have given any of these gentlemen reason to hope."

"None of them, ma'am."

"Not even the Marquis?"

"I am not ambitious for a title."

"And yet, my dear, if ever a woman was born to be a wife, I believe it to be you. You have a warm heart and you know how to create a home. I have watched how you have transformed your uncle, who can be such a curmudgeon, but he has flowered under your care."

"Well, I am very fond of him."

"Heaven knows how you can be," commented the Dowager caustically, "even though he is my oldest friend. You deserve something better than your present life."

"But I am perfectly happy as I am," Celina protested, trying to sound convincing. "Clearly I am destined to be an old maid."

"Stuff and nonsense! I have other plans for you."

"You have – ? No, please, Lady Torrington, I don't want you to try to find me a husband."

"Of course not. You have shown that you can do that for yourself. But finding the right husband is another matter. My dear, you have always been like a daughter to me."

"And you have been a second mother to me," Celina admitted warmly.

"I have tried to be. But now, I want to ask you to do something for me. It is something very dear to my heart."

"Then I will do it, ma'am. You know I am glad to do anything for you that I can. What is this favour?"

"Simply this. I want you to marry my son."

*

It was Robin's habit to rise early and take his breakfast alone, even if he had entertained company the night before. In his opinion, few women looked good in the harsh glare of early daylight.

He had experienced some difficulty evading Monique and Colette the next morning and it had wearied him of females for some days.

While he drank his coffee his mail was brought to him. One letter, he noticed, came from England and he opened it first.

It was from his mother's sister, Clarice, a lady of whom he was very fond, although he saw very little of her.

She wrote,

'Your dear Mama is the last person to complain, but the fact is that she is very weak and growing weaker with every day that passes. Her heart has never been strong and it would not surprise me to find that she does not have long to live.

There is just one favour she desires, Robin dear, and that is to see you.

She loves you very much and it has made her very sad that she has not seen you for several months.'

Robin rose sharply to his feet, his face clouded by concern. Despite his self-indulgent life he adored his mother and knew that, however much he was enjoying himself in Paris, he must return immediately to England.

He could have no peace of mind until he had seen her.

"Call my valet," he ordered the hovering footman. "Tell him to prepare for a speedy departure."

He dressed hurriedly and as he did so he gave a stream of instructions to his secretary.

"You will need to cancel all my social engagements," he said. "I am afraid there may be quite a number of them."

"Yes, my Lord," the secretary replied woodenly. "May I ask if there are any 'social engagements' lingering in the house at the moment?"

"No, damn your impudence! But you will need to write a lot of letters refusing invitations, making my apologies and such like, as I am called home to England by my mother's illness."

"Can I say when your Lordship intends to return to Paris?"

"I have no idea, but I will not stay away longer than necessary."

He recalled that his mother had always been delicate, but a new diet and the right medicine could strengthen her. He had no doubt that it would be the same this time.

He decided, therefore, to take only the bare minimum of luggage which meant five heavy cases.

At last the carriage arrived at his door and he climbed into it with Stigwood, his valet. A short ride took them to the railway station and from there it was a three-hour journey to Calais.

Here they were forced to stay the night, as a storm had blown up that kept the boats in port.

Having eaten a good dinner, drunk the excellent wine and flirted with the landlord's pretty daughter, Robin wandered out onto the seafront where the wind was blowing gustily.

The brilliant moon cast a silver glow on the turbulent waters beneath, giving the earth and sky a look of ghostly terror.

He stood there watching while the wind whipped his cloak about him and he found a kind of pleasure in the violence of the scene.

Looking at the wild night he found that his self-indulgent life seemed tame by contrast. The pleasures that came so easily because he always possessed the wherewithal to pay, the procession of willing women, the instant gratification of every whim – reluctant as he was to admit it, these were actually beginning to cloy.

Where were the mountains to climb? Where was the excitement that gave savour to life? Where was the challenge that could make his heart beat faster with the determination to overcome all obstacles in its pursuit?

He had everything a man could want – except something to long for.

He turned to make his way back to the hotel. Then he stopped in his tracks, alerted by something he had seen.

At least, he thought he had seen it.

He looked around him. He was alone.

For a moment he could have sworn there was another presence there, a face that he recognised, that he had last seen filled with hate.

Giving himself a little shake he returned to the hotel and ordered brandy to be served in his room.

"The storm's quietening a bit," Stigwood observed, folding clothes away and glancing out of the window. "We should be off tomorrow."

"Good. I am beginning to see ghosts in this place."

"What kind of ghosts, my Lord?"

"Things that cannot be there, like Pierre Vallon."

"The thief you put away two years ago?"

"That's right."

"I remember him cursing and swearing revenge," Stigwood said with relish. "Ah, but that was a splendid scene. Ten years he got, didn't he?"

"Yes. So he must still be behind bars and I cannot have seen him. Besides, if he had been there I am sure he would have tried to kill me."

"Oh, no, my Lord, he was planning something worse. Do you not remember that he said he'd do something that would break your heart? And one of them fine ladies said you had no heart."

"That's right," Robin remembered with relish. "I took her to bed that very night, as a token of my appreciation."

Stigwood grinned.

"With most gentlemen it's the other way round," he commented. "They want the women to think they do have a heart."

"More fool them! A wise man lays out his stall honestly so that they cannot complain. Goodnight Stigwood."

To his relief the storm had abated by next day and they were able to board ship. As it pulled away from the quay he looked back at the coast of France, wondering when he would see it again, hoping that it would not be too long.

But he knew that however great a pull Paris exerted on him, he must see first to his mother's welfare. Apart from his affection for her, he was truly grateful for the way she had run the Torrington estate so well, enabling him to spend so much of his life abroad.

Suddenly he grew very still, watching one particular face. A man stood on the quay, staring as the boat pulled away. There was a terrible stillness about him, and it seemed to Robin that, just as his own eyes were fixed on the man, so the man's eyes were trained on him.

And those eyes were full of terrible meaning.

"Look there," he called to Stigwood. "Do you see Pierre Vallon?"

"No," Stigwood replied, scanning the quay. "How could it be him when he's still in prison?"

"True," Robin agreed with a shrug.

When he looked again there was no sign of Vallon.

*

Robin reached Torrington Castle in the late afternoon and the first person he saw was the doctor coming downstairs.

"How is she?" he asked at once.

Dr. Thorell hesitated before saying cautiously,

"Let us just say that I am glad you are now here. Your mother is very weak –

"But she will recover," he continued tensely. "She's had bad turns before, but they pass. She is not a young woman and the present situation cannot last forever. I know there are things she wants to say to you while there is still time."

"Still time?" Robin echoed, aghast. "What the devil do you mean by that?"

The doctor's only answer was a look. It was enough to send him flying up the stairs and along the corridor to his mother's room.

"Mama!" he cried, bursting in, running to the bed and clasping his mother in his arms.

From her pillow she looked up at him mistily, eyes glowing with joy at seeing her son again.

"It's been so long," she murmured. "I was not expecting you."

"Aunt Clarice wrote to me that you were ill, so of course I came at once. You should have told me."

"My dear boy, I don't want to alarm you for every little thing. I have my funny turns, as you know."

"But you always recover quickly," he said. "This will be the same."

30

"I am not sure that it will. Something tells me that my illness is more serious this time. If you had not returned now, I was planning to send for you. I must speak to you seriously before I – "

She was stopped by her son's fingers laid quickly over her lips.

"Don't talk now," he urged. "We will have plenty of time later."

"I fear not. My dearest Robin, my time is running out. I cannot last much longer. Let me go to my grave knowing that all is well with you."

"But if you are not here, all cannot be well with me," he said fervently.

His mother smiled.

"I know, my darling," she answered. "But no one lives for ever and when I finally go to Heaven, I want to know that what I leave behind me is as safe and perfect in your hands as it has been in your father's.

"And that means that you must now do your duty, not only in looking after your great inheritance, but in founding a family to carry on into the next generation, and the next."

"Mama – "

"Yes, I know. I have often begged you to marry, have I not? And you have always asked me to be patient. But I can be patient no longer. Allow me the happiness of seeing you married before I die."

"But Mama, I have never found anyone that I wanted to make my wife."

"Of course not, because you are not looking in the right places. Now listen to me, darling."

Robin took her hand and kissed it.

"I am listening, Mama," he said.

"People of our rank cannot always hope to marry for

love and I think you will certainly never do so. You need a bride who is suitable and I have found her for you."

"Mama!"

"She is young and well-born, although not so well-born that she could ever outrank you. She has lived in this part of the country for several years and knows what will be required of her when she is Countess of Torrington."

"She lives here? Have I met her?"

"Of course. She is Celina Storton, whom I know you like."

"*Celina*?" he repeated stupidly.

"Celina. The best possible choice in the world. She already knows the worst of you, so you will not come as too much of an unpleasant surprise!"

"Unpleasant?"

"Well, my dear boy, your reputation is hardly of the best, but she knows you well enough to make allowances."

"Very kind of her."

"Yes, and you should be grateful, for you need a woman who will be kind to you and not mind too much if you try her patience."

"Mama, what an extraordinary idea!"

"It is an excellent idea and you will come to believe so too."

He was silent for a moment and then he burst out laughing.

"Celina?" he echoed. "Me, marry Celina? No really, that is *too* much!"

He carried himself off into another burst of hilarity. His mother watched, exasperated, waiting for him to stop.

But he did not stop. Instead he laughed and laughed and laughed.

CHAPTER THREE

For some time after her talk with the Dowager, Celina wanted only to be alone with her thoughts. What she had heard and what she had said in reply was so momentous, that she could not bear anyone else's company.

"*I want you to marry my son.*"

That was what the Dowager Countess had said and for a moment Celina's heart had leapt. After all this time he wanted her and had asked his mother to make the proposal for him.

But then her delicious haze had cleared and she had realised that he knew nothing about this idea. It was not he who wanted her, but the Dowager, anxious to see him settle down.

"Ma'am, please stop and think," she had said when she could control her sick disappointment. "He will never allow you to choose his wife."

"He will never choose one for himself if I don't act soon. I am persuaded that Robin will not marry for love. He has too many strange notions about love and marriage.

"Very well. Let him marry for friendship. Some of the best unions are made that way. And what woman is a better friend to him than you?"

Celina was silent, tormented equally by hope and doubt.

"I do not pretend that it will always be easy," the Dowager continued carefully. "We both know what he is like and he is certainly not going to change overnight."

"You mean he will not be faithful, ma'am?" Celina asked bluntly.

"It is not part of any man's nature to be faithful, even when they do marry for love," the Dowager replied. "We must be realistic. There is much to be said for harbouring no illusions on your wedding day. It saves a great deal of heartbreak later."

"So I imagine," Celina murmured wryly.

"And you are a sensible girl. I know I can entrust him to you. And you can run the estate for him, as I have done."

"Thus enabling him to return to Paris and leave me alone?" Celina queried lightly. "I thought you said he was beginning to recognise his obligations?"

"He is indeed," she declared with more hope than conviction. "He knows he must have children, and I am sure that whenever he departs for France you will always be with child."

She seemed to find nothing wrong with this picture, so Celina forbore to say that it sounded a very bleak marriage. She merely observed,

"I will need time to think about this, ma'am."

"Of course, my dear. But I am sure that when you have considered everything you will see what an excellent notion it is. You will have a fine home, rank and children. Better that than be a lonely old maid. Also," she added hopefully, "as Robin grows older, he will probably slow down a bit."

'Slowing down' would probably mean chasing females in this neighbourhood. Of the two Celina thought she might prefer Paris.

She had returned home sunk in thought. Her first thought was to reject the proposal utterly. She loved Robin with all her heart and soul.

She had dreamed of seeing the light of love in his eyes, of standing beside him in Church as he slipped a ring on her finger and made her his wife.

Now she was offered the loveless shadow of her dream – to become his wife, knowing that she meant nothing to him.

How could she endure it?

But then she thought of the life that lay before her if she refused.

She knew that her uncle would not live for very many more years. She would inherit his property which was comfortable but not luxurious and then spend the rest of her days alone.

Perhaps, in time, she would see the man she loved wed to another woman and still wish she had taken the chance when it was offered.

She would be lonely and often jealously miserable, but she would be the mother of his children. She could seek her happiness in them.

And perhaps, in time, her husband might become attached to her. It was little enough, but it was more than she had dared to hope for.

After two days of torment and indecision she returned to Torrington Castle.

"I will do as you wish, ma'am," she agreed quietly.

"I knew you would, my dear."

This made Celina feel, wryly, that it would be better if the Dowager had not been quite so certain. But, as the most important lady in the district, she was used to being able to order everyone's life, except her son's.

As if she could read her young friend's mind, the Dowager said placatingly,

"I meant only that I know how sensible you are. And this is really the most sensible choice to make, both for you and for him. Good sense is always best – in the end."

Good sense. With those two words she dismissed the dreams that had brightened Celina's life for years. She would attain her goal while losing the very thing that made it beautiful.

"Yes, ma'am," she said quietly. "I am sure you are right."

"Good, now everything is settled, we must start to make plans."

"But surely, everything is not settled? Your son still has to agree to this marriage. Perhaps he will not want to marry me?"

The Dowager smiled.

"You can leave that to me," she stated firmly. "Yes, what is it?"

The question was addressed to a footman who entered the room bearing a silver tray, on which lay a letter, the envelope of which was addressed in a very large, distinctive writing. Celina, who had seen it before, recognised the hand of her Ladyship's sister, Clarice.

Evidently the Dowager also recognised it, for she seized up the letter with a little mutter of pleasure and tore it open. After reading a few lines she tossed it aside apparently pleased with what she had read.

"Now," she said, "I want you to talk to my dresser about your wedding gown. She tends to every detail of my appearance, mending, lace-making and sometimes designing clothes. She has your dress all planned."

"I am sure she has," Celina murmured, in a daze.

"Then off you go. She is upstairs."

Celina bent to retrieve the letter which had fallen on the floor. Without meaning too, she could not help reading the first line.

'*I have done just as you instructed –* '

Hastily she set the letter on a low table, careful not to read any more and hurried from the room.

She was not really surprised to discover that Mrs. Ragley, the dresser, had prepared some sketches and chosen the material, a glorious white satin. The veil was a Torrington family heirloom.

"Yes, I guessed your size perfectly," Mrs. Ragley enthused. "It won't take me long to finish the dress."

"Will you need me to come for a fitting?"

"Yes, but not for a day or two. Don't worry, I will send for you when I am ready."

Celina went meekly away and did not return until she received Mrs. Ragley's summons two days later.

Within ten minutes she was on her way in the pony and trap.

No matter how hard she tried to cling to common sense, she was filled with delight. She was going to try on her wedding dress for the ceremony that would make her Robin's wife, as she had always dreamed of being. How could she be anything but happy?

And when she reached the castle there was something else to increase her joy. A carriage stood at the front door and there, pulling out the baggage, was Stigwood, the Earl's valet.

So he had come home. Suddenly her heart was full to overflowing and she began to hurry. The front door stood wide open and she was too well known in the house for anyone to challenge her, so that she was able to run directly up the stairs to the Dowager's room.

But when she reached her door she stopped, held back by a sudden shyness. Robin might be in there, talking to his mother. How would she face him?

Suddenly she tensed, alerted by the sound of male laughter, coming from just behind the door which stood slightly ajar. It was Robin and he was clearly enjoying a very good joke.

At last he paused in his laughter.

"Celina?" he queried in a voice that held as much astonishment as amusement.

She drew in her breath, her heart pounding as she waited for what he would say about her. At last he continued,

"Me, marry Celina? No really, that is *too* much!"

He began to laugh again and this time he did not stop. Celina listened, frozen, as the sound of his mirth seemed to stream out, surrounding her, causing her to choke.

"Mama, what were you thinking of?" he demanded. "Celina's a nice girl, but she's been on the shelf for *years*."

"She is twenty-five," came his mother's acid voice.

"I rest my case."

"Twenty-five is not old."

"It is if you are a countrified spinster."

"On the contrary, she has recently returned from London where, I understand, she received several good proposals."

"Did she tell you that?" he asked hilariously. "Poor Celina. She's been unlucky, so I suppose she has to invent these tales."

Celina gasped and put her hands to her mouth to choke back the tide of misery.

Then she heard his footsteps coming closer to the door. Her heart thundered with dread. He must not find her here.

38

Quick as a flash she turned and darted down the stairs, out of the front door and towards the stables.

In another moment she was in the trap, frantically urging the pony to take her home as soon as possible.

Afterwards she could never remember anything about that journey. She knew that her heart was breaking and she would gladly die, but she saw nothing of the road flowing beneath her or the trees fleeing past.

If only she could reach home quickly and lock herself away where nobody could ever see her again. She thought the road would go on forever, but at last she could turn into the yard and halt sharply.

Tossing the reins to a groom, she flew upstairs and threw herself onto the bed, sobbing her heart out.

*

"Mama, you really must forget this idea," Robin said when he managed to stop laughing. "I am not ready to be wed."

"I did not ask if you were ready. I ask you to give me the dearest wish of my heart before – before it is too late."

His laughter faded abruptly. Something about his mother's voice told him that things had changed.

"If I have to die," she said, "and it may be very soon, I want to be sure that the Torrington family will carry on, in pride and honour, for many more generations."

Robin bent down and kissed her cheek.

"I will do my best, Mama. I want you to be happy but I also want you, as you have always been, to be here looking after me and loving me, as I love you so much."

"Yes, you do love me, I know," she said, "and you would not want me to die unhappy."

"I wish you wouldn't keep talking about dying," he said in alarm. "I am sure you are worrying about nothing."

But then he remembered the doctor's face and how gravely he had spoken and he felt uneasy.

He wanted to please her, but how could he possibly do what she asked?

He had expected his mother to have much to say to him when he returned home, but never in his wildest dreams did he think for one moment she would have arranged his marriage and found him a wife in his absence.

He was about to say that the whole idea was impossible, but then his mother said weakly,

"I do not expect, my dearest son, to live for very long. The doctor has told me there is nothing he can do and now I must think of what will happen after I am gone.

"It has been my dream to see you happily married to a nice girl with your children growing around you. Alas, I shall not see my grandchildren, but I can at least witness your wedding.

"Then I shall know that the grandeur and traditions of our house are safe with you and that our line will go on and on, becoming more and more glorious. But perhaps I ask too much."

Her voice died away and Robin could not, for the moment, find anything to say.

He could only stare at her, thinking that it was impossible to do what she had requested. Even for her, he would not give up his freedom.

But then he realised how fragile she looked.

Could it really be true, what she was saying, that she would not live for very much longer?

It might even kill her now if he refused to do what she wanted. How could he face life with that stain on his conscience?

He had been selfish all his life, but he was not heartless

and he loved his mother.

With an effort which seemed to him to come from the very depths of his body, he said,

"Very well, Mama. I will do as you ask."

"Oh, thank you, my son, thank you with all my heart. You have made your mother so very happy."

In an ecstasy of relief she threw her arms around him. He hugged her back, truly moved.

"But of course," he added, "it depends on whether Celina is willing."

"How can you doubt it?" she asked with a faint touch of acid. "You seem to think that she is at her last prayers."

"Well, I certainly don't believe the story of her fighting off suitors. So you think she will be ready to put up with me, having no other offers?"

"A girl must make do with whoever she can find." She eyed him. "However unimpressive."

There was an ironic gleam in her eye that made him grin. It did not occur to him that it contrasted oddly with her feeble manner.

"Quite so, Mama! And I suppose there might be advantages to having a wife who knows me so well."

"Yes, you won't have to make pretty speeches or tell the usual lies," she observed caustically.

Then she gave a sigh.

"Tonight I will dine in my room and you will join me. But leave me for now. I am weary."

Silently he vowed that he would do whatever was necessary to please his mother while she was alive. He would marry and remain here, a devoted son and a respectable husband, as long as she wanted him.

But all his senses were telling him that this would not be for long. And then he would return to his true life in Paris.

Later that evening, as she had said, the Dowager and her son dined in her room.

"Since you seem to have everything planned you had better tell me what happens next," he enquired mildly, pouring her a glass of wine. "Shall I visit Celina or is she coming to us?"

"I was rather hoping to see her today. Mrs. Ragley is making her dress and sent for her for a fitting. But she says Celina did not arrive."

"She is making her dress?" he echoed. "You were very sure of my answer, were you not?"

"I want no delay to this wedding."

"And if you had to choose some other bride, no doubt the dress could be altered to fit her," he observed with a smile. "Mama, you are incorrigible."

"Certainly I am. Nothing would ever be done in this place otherwise."

"Perhaps Celina does not want to marry me?"

"Half of me wishes that were true. It would do you the world of good. However, you had better visit her tomorrow and settle the matter."

His eyes gleamed with humour.

"Yes, Mama. No, Mama. Whatever you say, Mama."

"Don't be impertinent."

*

Celina rose early next morning and, taking pen and paper, sat down by her bedroom window. Her head was aching from a sleepless night and her face was wet with tears as she wrote a brief letter to the Dowager.

She wrote

'Forgive me, but I am unable to do as your Ladyship wishes. Mature reflection has convinced me that such a marriage could not succeed.

I hope you will manage to find a wife for Lord Torrington. His rank and wealth will always make him most eligible and there must be many females who will overlook his reputation, and various other matters, in return for those qualities.'

She signed the letter,

'Your affectionate friend,

Celina Storton.'

Then she sent it off by a footman, hoping it would arrive during breakfast. Her Ladyship would read it and almost certainly show it to her son.

Celina experienced an angry pleasure at the thought of Robin reading those last few lines.

Let him know that she spurned him, that he was no more than a reject, shopping for a wife among women whose desperation would make them settle for anything – even him.

Yes, even him, she thought, her anger subsiding into wistfulness. Even him, with his wickedly enticing smile, the devilish charm in his eyes, his taut, upright figure, his way of looking the world in the face and daring it to do its worst.

Yes, *even him.*

Then she pulled herself together and forced herself to remember the real situation. It was she who was the reject, a woman who could make the man she adored roar with laughter at the mere thought of marrying her. And she had better not forget it.

After that she concentrated on her day's work and was settled in the library, going over the household accounts, when a cab drew up outside the door.

The angle of the house cut off her view, so she could not see the new arrival until the library door burst open and a voice, throbbing with melodrama, cried,

"There you are!"

"My Lord!" she exclaimed, jumping to her feet, astonished at the sight of Lord Delaine. "What are you doing here?"

The Marquis waddled into the room, puffing mightily.

"I came for you, Goddess!" he cried. "Picture my sensations when I discovered that you had fled. Imagine my anguish, my heartbreak!"

"I tried to make you understand – "

But he was in full flight and too absorbed in his own drama to listen to her.

"'It cannot be!' I cried. 'But so it was.' You had gone, and I was desolate."

Despite her unhappiness Celina could not suppress a smile. She hastily covered her mouth, but she was not in time.

"You laugh at me," the Marquis shouted.

"No, truly – "

"You scorn my passion, but I have a heart only for you. Let me lay it once more at your feet."

"Please, you must not – "

But he was already well into his rehearsed performance, drooping down onto one knee, just as before, producing the same diamond ring and seizing her hand.

"Look at it," he cried. "Have you ever seen a ring like this one? So elegant. So *large!* How the other women will envy you! Think how you will take precedence over them – well, most of them."

She had thought such an argument could never sway her, but into her mind suddenly came the memory of Robin's laughter and his voice saying cruelly,

'Celina's a nice girl, but she's been on the shelf for years.'

Rank. Title. Precedence. She had never cared for any

of them before, but now she remembered that a *Marquis* outranked an *Earl*.

So she was a countrified spinster, was she?

It would be – a pleasure to teach him a lesson.

When she was a Marchioness, he could never laugh at her again.

It would be so easy. She had only to allow Lord Delaine to slide the ring onto her finger – just as he was doing now –

She stared down at the huge diamond on her left hand, wondering how it had got there.

"You accept me!" Delaine cried. "This is more than I dared to hope. I swear you will never regret it."

"My Lord," Celina stammered, "I cannot – please – do not – "

She was barely conscious of what she was saying. The dazzling vision of making Robin eat his words was so strong that for a moment she almost felt that she might throw caution to the winds, accept the Marquis and queen it over London Society.

Emboldened, the Marquis struggled to his feet and seized her in his arms.

"Mine!" he howled. *"Mine!"*

She raised her arms to fend him off, but it was a mistake because it enabled him to slip his hands around her waist, draw her close and plant his lips on her mouth.

She tried to struggle but she could do little except thump his shoulders while trying vainly to free her mouth.

She began to feel desperate, unable to call for help.

Then she heard noises, footsteps, an angry oath and suddenly the Marquis was gone, hauled off her by forceful hands.

The shock was so sudden that Celina staggered back

and landed, sprawling on the sofa.

Next she saw the man who had come to her rescue.

It was Robin!

She could have screamed.

"Let me go," the Marquis shrieked, trying to wriggle free from Robin's painful grasp on his ear.

"First you have some explaining to do," hissed Robin, still holding him.

"How dare you!" the Marquis roared. "This lady is my promised wife and if I choose to kiss her it is none of your business."

"Your promised wife?" Robin questioned cynically.

"If you don't believe me, look at her left hand. That ring is a family heirloom. My grandfather gave it to my grandmother and my father gave it to my mother."

The sight of the ring made Robin pause long enough for the Marquis to twist himself free.

"And now I have given it to my bride," he announced breathlessly. "I begged her to be my wife and when she consented, I slipped it on her finger. There it will lie until I add a wedding ring to it and she becomes the Marchioness of Delaine."

At last Celina found her voice.

"No – forgive me, my Lord, but – "

"You will make the finest Marchioness in London," he squawked, oblivious to everything but his own transports. "The happiest moment of my life was when you said you would be mine."

Robin was watching Celina narrowly.

"Is that what you said?" he asked.

"No, I never meant – "

She was struggling with the ring but it was stuck.

Some glimmer of the truth was beginning to reach the Marquis.

"I will cover you with jewels," he gasped. "You will enjoy the friendship of Royalty – "

"Stop talking like a ninny," Robin cut in bluntly.

Moving quickly he seized Celina's hand, removed the huge diamond ring and tossed it to the rejected suitor.

A moment of farce then ensued as the ring slithered away, forcing the Marquis to dive under a sofa searching for it.

Robin contemplated the Marquis's large rear and his foot twitched.

"Tempting," he said. "But a waste of time. Get up man and be off. You have had your chance."

The Marquis emerged dishevelled, clutching the ring and scrambled to his feet.

"Ahah!" he cried. "False woman! You have deceived me."

"I never deceived you," Celina replied indignantly.

"You swore that there was no other man. You lied. You love another!"

"I most certainly do not. I do not love Lord Torrington any more than I love you, and I am not marrying either of you. Please leave at once."

For a moment it looked as if the Marquis might stand his ground, but a glance at Robin's grim face seemed to change his mind. He gave a sketchy bow to Celina and scampered away.

"Now, madam," Robin said, turning to her. "I believe we have business to discuss."

CHAPTER FOUR

Celina could hear a strange singing in her ears. The whole world seemed to be throbbing around her.

The scene that had just passed should have left her devastated, embarrassed, horrified.

Instead she felt ablaze with brilliant life.

He had called her a countrified spinster, *'on the shelf for years'*. He had sneered and laughed at her and accused her of inventing tales about men proposing to her.

Well, *now* he knew.

He had seen the Marquis of Delaine at her feet and seen the Delaine diamond on her finger. And he had heard her reject, not only Delaine, but himself.

She had fought back and whatever happened after this, for one blinding glorious moment she had known an excitement that was greater than anything in her life.

She could face him with her head held high and that was what she would do.

"I am obliged to you, my Lord," she ventured, confronting him, "for coming to my rescue. I had thought that the Marquis had accepted my refusal, but it seems not."

"Yes, he must be very much in love to have pursued you here," Robin observed. "I understand that he is not alone in his passion. Do you anticipate any other interruptions?"

"I think not."

"Good. Then we can talk. Do you mind telling me what lay behind the note you sent to my mother this morning? It upset her a good deal."

"I am so sorry for that and I shall apologise to her personally. But I do not believe that she can seriously have expected me to marry you."

"She was certainly under the impression that you had agreed."

"Your mother is my oldest and dearest friend. When she made her request, my first thought was that I would do anything for her. But naturally, on reflection, I realised that it was impossible. You must surely have come to the same conclusion, so we are bound to be in agreement."

"I am not concerned with your refusal, but with the fact that you failed to make your feelings clear from the beginning."

"That was careless of me, but I was taken by surprise. Had I had time to think I would have told your mother that I have no taste for the married state. I am, after all, twenty-five years old, an age at which most ladies have married.

"Those that are still unwed have either had no chances or have chosen to embrace the single state. You have seen for yourself which one is true in my case."

It might have been her imagination that he reddened slightly. It was hard to be sure since he quickly looked away. No matter. She was enjoying herself.

"I pity any woman who has no choice but to enter the yoke of matrimony," she continued. "She is condemned forever to endure her husband's temper. True happiness is only to be found in freedom. I shall remain my own mistress and consult only my own wishes."

"I see. You envision marriage as mere servitude?"

"For a woman, yes. The man, of course, does as he

pleases, absents himself when he so desires, comes home when he pleases and discourages questions."

Since this was precisely his notion of the perfect marriage, it was unreasonable of Robin to be annoyed, but he found his ire growing, nonetheless.

"You consider all men monsters?"

"Not *all*," she said, apparently considering. "Uncle James, for instance, is an excellent gentleman."

"Your Uncle James is a dried-up old stick," he snapped.

"That *may* help," she conceded.

"He is also nearly invisible. You practically never see him."

"As I say, an excellent man."

"You are irrational, my dear Celina. One of your complaints against husbands is that they absent themselves too often. The same quality in your uncle rouses your approval."

"But my uncle is not my husband. A husband owes his wife at least the appearance of pleasure at her company, and, for this, it is helpful if he spends some time with her. Well, in most cases, anyway!"

Some note in her voice warned Robin that she was about to say something outrageous, and he knew he would be wise to leave the subject at that point. But for the life of him he could not stop himself saying,

"May I ask exactly what you mean by that, madam?"

"Well, if I was to be so foolish as to marry you, for instance, I would make not the least objection to your absence."

"In fact the less you saw of me the better?"

"That is a rather harsh way of putting it for, be assured, I bear you no ill will."

"You are very kind," he said ironically.

"But since, once married, we would spend as much time apart as we do now, such a marriage would be pointless."

"Except that it is my mother's dearest wish."

"It is her dearest wish to see you settled down, not necessarily with me. You will have no difficulty choosing another bride somewhere else."

"Ah, yes," he retorted with a touch of savagery, "a female who will overlook 'other things' for the sake of my rank and wealth. But did you have to insult me in a letter to my mother?"

So he had read her letter, just as she had meant him to do. She was so delighted that she hastily covered her mouth with her hands in well-simulated horror.

"You read it? Oh, you should not have done."

"My mother showed it to me," he raged. "She said I had brought your censure on myself."

"Oh, how could she?" Celina moaned. "My words were meant for her eyes alone."

"Whoever they were meant for, what the devil did you mean by them? Do you think I have to go out begging in the highways and byways to find a wife?"

"Well, you haven't found one so far," she replied with spirit. "Rank and wealth notwithstanding."

"When I wish to marry, madam, I shall choose my own wife and she – "

Belatedly he recalled what had brought him here.

"Never mind that," he said hastily. "It is pointless to continue this discussion. You are the bride my mother has chosen."

She gave a trill of disbelieving laughter.

"And you will let her foist her choice on you? Fie, sir!

51

What weakness is this? Be a man. Insist on your own way, as I believe you always do."

She had the satisfaction of seeing him totally bereft of words.

Oh, revenge was sweet!

He took a deep breath before speaking again in the manner of a man restraining himself with great difficulty.

"All this would be very much to the point were it not for the fact that my mother is extremely ill, and unlikely to live for long."

Her amusement faded and she turned to face him in horror.

"Oh, no, I cannot believe it. When we spoke the other day she seemed the same as usual. Of course I have never known her to be robust, but she was not worse, I am sure of it."

"She has been frail for years, but she has concealed the severity of her condition," he said gruffly. "Now she is at death's door and I feel that I must do as she wants, as long as she is alive."

"I did not know," Celina whispered.

Suddenly the situation was no longer a joke or a subject for revenge. Her dear friend was dying.

"I must go and see her at once," she said.

"And break her heart by refusing her dearest wish?" Robin demanded. "I will not take you to her if you are going to do that."

"But – how can I tell what I am going to say?" she stammered. "You have taken me by surprise – "

"You knew what she wanted days ago."

"But not this – oh, what am I to do?"

"I had not realised that the thought of marrying me was so terrible."

"You are hardly the ideal husband," she flashed. "A woman would have to be mad – "

"Say no more," he said curtly. "You have made your opinion of me all too plain. I had thought we were friends."

"Friends, yes. But marriage is different."

"You were willing to consider that booby Delaine."

"I was not," she replied hotly. "I wanted nothing to do with him."

"You forget that I found you in his arms, his ring on your finger. How did it get there? Against your will? I don't think so. You are quite capable of boxing his ears before he even seized your hand."

"How dare you!" she shouted in outrage. "If you have the unbelievable impertinence to suggest that I encouraged him – "

"Let us say that you did not refuse his proposal with that wholehearted finality that would have prevented him from following you."

"Stuff and nonsense!" she said crisply

Robin stared. It was safe to say that nobody had spoken to him like this for years. Certainly not a young woman.

"Nothing could have stopped him following me," Celina declared. "He simply cannot accept that any woman can resist what he has to offer. I believe there are many such men. They are exceedingly tiresome."

The last words were delivered with a challenging air, directed straight to him, in a manner that was unmistakeable.

"In that case, it is fortunate that I appeared on the scene when I did," he said harshly. "Or you might have ended up the Marchioness of Delaine, despite your resistance. As it is, you are free to marry me and so bring my mother peace and happiness in her last few weeks."

His words stopped Celina in her tracks. In her annoyance with him, she had almost forgotten the sad fact that had brought him here.

Now she was faced with a decision. And she was torn. On the one hand was her pride. On the other hand was her affection for the Dowager and her feelings for her son.

She might deny it all she pleased, but her love for Robin endured. Marriage to him would bring her both pain and joy. And which would be the greater, she could not imagine.

"I do not know – " she whispered. "I do not know – "

He took a step towards her.

"Then perhaps this will help you decide," he said roughly and pulled her round to face him.

At first she barely realised what he meant to do.

She had one glimpse of his face, dark with impatience and some other mysterious feeling, before he pulled her close and lowered his head until his lips touched hers.

She gave a gasp at the sudden sensation. It was like being burned and she felt a spurt of temper at the way he took for granted that he could do as he liked.

"How dare you!" she spluttered, struggling. "Let me go at once or I shall slap your face."

"You didn't slap Delaine," he murmured against her lips. "Don't tell me that you prefer his embrace to mine."

Before she could reply he tightened his arms, so that she was pulled against him in a crushing embrace. His mouth was hard on hers, kissing her fiercely, ruthlessly.

She knew all about his reputation that he was an expert lover, skilled at bringing women under his spell.

Now she found that it was true.

There was devilment in his lips. They knew how to move over a woman's mouth, coaxing a response from her, inciting fires of pleasure that threatened to overwhelm her.

She could feel herself melting, wanting only him, ready to set the world at nothing if only she could be held in his arms. The warmth was spreading through her body, terrifying her with its power to undermine her will.

She would not give in, *she would not –*

It took a superhuman effort, but when he released her she knew that he could have had little inkling of the storm of feeling that left her dizzy.

She had resisted the temptation to put her arms round him, drawing him closer to her, seeking deeper intimacy, more passionate caresses. She had stood tense and rigid while he teased and taunted her with his lips and his hands.

Now there was the inevitable reaction. She was almost fainting, but she forced herself to step back and face him with her head up, her eyes full of defiance.

"Well, my Lord?" she challenged in a voice that only just managed to be steady. "Have you proved something? Have you succeeded in flattering your own vanity?"

"Is that your way of saying that you will not marry me?"

"No, my Lord. It is my way of saying that I will marry you for your mother's sake and *only* for her sake. You will not reduce me to your willing slave, as I hear you do with so many others."

"You listen to too much gossip," he said curtly.

"I do not need to. You flaunt your conquests in the most vulgar manner, but I will not be one of them. Understand that and we may deal well together."

"By Heaven, madam, you are very sure of yourself, making conditions!"

"It is you who wants this marriage, my Lord. Not me."

For a moment he was so tense that she thought he

would burst into a furious tirade against her. Then the anger seemed to drain out of him and his shoulders slumped.

"Yes, I do," he said heavily. "And I am asking you to do what will make my mother happy and become my wife."

"On that understanding, I will marry you."

The words were said. For both of them there would be no going back.

But neither of them could imagine what the future held.

"Now, let us go to see your mother," she suggested, glad to find something to say. "And tell her some news that will make her feel better."

He had arrived in the Torrington carriage and they travelled back in it together. On the way he discussed the coming nuptials in a brisk way that was almost businesslike.

Part of her was sad that the wedding that had filled her dreams was reduced to this unemotional arrangement. Yet part of her was glad. Keeping matters cool would help her stay in control.

It seemed as though the news had gone around the household, so that when they drew up outside Torrington Castle and Robin gave her his hand to help her down from the carriage, all the servants were pressed against the windows, eagerly gazing down.

There was another face at an upstairs window, but the Dowager drew back hastily before her son could look up and see her. Her face was full of anxiety as she made her way slowly back to her bed and lay down.

From her dressing gown pocket she drew the letter that Celina had sent her that morning, breaking off the engagement, and read it again. Then she closed her eyes and prayed with all her might.

After a moment there was a light knock on the door

before Celina's head appeared. At once she ran into the room, darting towards the bed.

"My dear ma'am, forgive me if I have upset you," she said fervently. "I did not mean to do so. I had no idea that you were so ill."

"I am sorry to be troublesome," the Dowager sighed weakly. "Ah, Robin, my dear boy!"

She held out her hand to him as he had entered the room behind Celina and now approached the bed.

"It is all right, Mama," he said. "Celina had doubts about such a hasty arrangement, but we have had a long talk and I think I have calmed her fears."

"That was all it was?" the Dowager asked anxiously.

"Indeed, ma'am, that is all," Celina said, as cheerfully as she could.

"We have been friends for so long that she thinks she could put up with me after all," Robin added.

"Truly?" the Dowager breathed, looking from one to the other, and clutching Celina's hand tightly. *"Truly?"*

"Truly," Celina replied.

"You will marry him? Let me hear you say it."

Celina raised her head and found Robin watching her. For what seemed like an eternity their eyes met. Then Celina said quietly,

"I will marry him."

The Countess fell back against her pillow.

"Thank Heavens!" she sighed. "Now I can die happy."

"I beg you not to talk of dying," Celina urged.

"But I must. I am old and ill and long to see my son settled with a good wife. My dear, I know you are the right person. Do not delay the wedding. Let it be as soon as possible."

"As soon as you wish," Celina agreed.

"It must be held in our private Chapel. I will send for the Vicar at once and explain everything to him. And you, my dear, must now have a fitting for your dress if it is to be ready in time."

Celina agreed. She was becoming dazed with the speed at which events were moving and the way everything was being taken out of her hands.

"But before you go," the Dowager continued weakly, "there is one more thing."

As they watched she drew her wedding ring from her finger, followed by her engagement ring with its huge sapphire surrounded by little diamonds.

"This ring has never left me," she murmured, "since the tenth Earl put it on my finger on the day of our betrothal. Now it will be yours. Let me see you wear it."

She handed it to her son. Solemnly he took Celina's left hand in his and slid the ring up her finger.

"Now you will be my wife," he said quietly.

She gazed at the ring, wondering how this could be happening.

A wave of emotion threatened to engulf her, but she fought it down, knowing that she must stay in command of herself or she would be swept away by her feelings.

"Yes, I shall be your wife," she agreed in the same sombre voice.

"My son, you should kiss her," the Dowager suggested wistfully.

"Not today, ma'am," Celina said quickly. "Until the wedding I am not truly a bride."

"Be patient, Mama," Robin said, in a more gentle voice than Celina had ever heard him use before.

He leaned down and kissed his mother on the cheek.

Watching him, Celina realised that this was the one woman that he truly loved. His manner to her was tender and full of warmth. It was like seeing a different man, and she thought wistfully that she would like to meet this other side of him. But it seemed that he kept it only for his mother.

She left them hurriedly and walked upstairs to where Mrs. Ragley was anxious to fit the dress onto her.

When everything was in place she looked at herself in the mirror and could hardly believe what she saw.

Could this vision in white satin and lace really be herself? Could such a dreamy, romantic-looking bride really be the woman who was about to enter an arranged marriage with a man who did not love her?

There was a knock on the door.

"May I come in?" came Robin's voice.

Mrs. Ragley gave a little shriek.

"No, my Lord! You must not see the bridal gown before the big day."

She ran and stood with her back to the door, ready to repel all-comers.

It gave Celina a weird feeling of unreality to see the conventions being strictly observed, as though this was a normal wedding.

But she, too, did not want him to see her gown before she walked down the aisle.

*

When she had hurriedly changed, Robin escorted her home and asked to see her uncle.

"I need to ask his permission to marry you," he announced grandly.

Uncle James, drawn away from some fascinating research in his library, seemed a little bemused by the question and indeed by the whole situation.

"You have already agreed?" he asked Celina.

"Yes, uncle. I have agreed to marry him and I hope you will give me away."

"Oh, well – of course, if it's all arranged. You must let me know when you settle the date."

"The day after tomorrow," Robin informed him.

"Oh, dear me, I am afraid I cannot manage that. I have several engagements scheduled for that day."

"One o'clock in the afternoon, in the private Chapel of Torrington Castle," Robin continued remorselessly. "I shall look forward to seeing you."

And thus he disposed of anyone or anything that might dissent to his plans, Celina thought wryly. She too had tried to dissent, and he had overcome her with a kiss whose apparent passion had not quite hidden the cynical ruthlessness lying beneath.

"Ah," said Uncle James. "I suppose, in that case, I had better be there."

That was his only comment, except to ask Celina anxiously that night,

"Is this really what you want, my dear?"

"Yes, dear uncle. I am quite content."

"Well, it is a good marriage, although such a quiet ceremony is hardly the way I thought to see you wed."

"It is only because the Dowager Countess is ill. She may die at any moment, so everything has to be completed in a rush."

"Yes, but the future Countess of Torrington deserves a big ceremony in the sight of the whole neighbourhood. Not a little service in a private Chapel, with only a couple of people there. But if you are happy with this arrangement, there is no more to be said."

"Of course I am happy. I am not a glowing young

bride, but an old maid, 'on the shelf for years' and grateful to seize her last chance," she replied in a teasing voice.

"On the shelf for years?" he echoed. "Nonsense! Who would dare to make such a remark?"

"Nobody," she answered, "but muted celebrations are most suitable for this occasion."

On the next day Mrs. Ragley delivered her dress and announced that she would stay overnight and dress her the next day. This caused Celina's maid, Agnes, to take furious offence, but Mrs. Ragley only sniffed. Clearly she did not consider Agnes up to the job of dressing a future Countess.

Eventually they settled on a truce and attired the bride together. Her bouquet was fresh flowers plucked from the garden that morning, and on her head were the famous Torrington pearls, sent over by the Dowager.

Despite her common sense words to her uncle, Celina felt a lifting of her heart when she surveyed herself in the mirror.

When Robin saw her advancing towards him down the aisle, surely he would see her with new eyes?

The future could be happy for them and together they might yet find love.

"My dear," her uncle said, "I have never seen you looking so glorious. It is as though you have a light shining from within you."

"I feel as though I have," she exclaimed joyfully. "Oh, Uncle James, I feel as though today is truly the beginning of a new and wonderful life."

"In that case," he said, giving her his arm, "let us go forward to your new life without delay."

Together they walked down the stairs, eagerly watched by all the servants who had gathered to wish her well, then out of the main doors into the glittering sunlight on her way to the beginning of her new happiness.

CHAPTER FIVE

As they turned into the gates of the castle Celina saw, with a shock, that the driveway was crowded with carriages. It seemed incredible that, in such a short time, invitations had been sent out and accepted.

Of course, she thought, nobody would want to miss the wedding of Lord Torrington, even at the last minute.

A powdered footman descended the steps to open the door of their carriage and usher them inside. Celina was dazzled by the profusion of flowers that were festooned everywhere.

A gentleman appeared whom Celina recognised as Lord Michael Ashley, Robin's second cousin, and now seemingly acting as unofficial host. He smiled, greeted her and shook her uncle's hand.

"Perhaps I should go upstairs to see her Ladyship before we start," she suggested.

"The Dowager Countess is waiting in the Chapel," Lord Michael informed her.

"I thought she was too ill to leave her bed."

"She had herself brought downstairs in a wheelchair. She said that nothing could make her miss Robin's nuptials."

"Of course. Then we must certainly not keep her waiting."

She thought how brave of the Dowager to insist on being present.

Lord Michael led them to the Chapel at the side of the castle, opened the door a crack and looked in.

He must have given a signal, because at once the organ began to play, "*Here comes the bride.*"

"Ready?" Uncle James whispered.

"Quite ready."

The door was flung open. She had a confused view of the Chapel, the aisle stretching before her up to the altar, and then it was time to move.

As she glided in and began the journey to where Robin was waiting, she realised that the Chapel must be much larger than she had ever appreciated.

It was packed with people as far as the eye could see.

Mostly they were a blur, but now and then her eye could pick out faces. There was Viscountess Carolmaine, once Lady Violet Manyard, who had schemed to marry Robin herself, until Celina had alerted him to the danger.

Marriage had not improved her temper if her chagrined expression was anything to go by.

But she had no time to waste on Violet. Her great moment was approaching, when she would become the wife of the man she adored.

Like a majestic white swan she floated down the aisle to the altar. Now she could see the Dowager, smiling as she watched the bride approach.

And there was Robin, standing very still and tense, his eyes fixed on the vision in white satin that was slowly coming towards him. And his expression was of a man who had received a stunning shock.

Celina's heart lifted. This was what she had longed for, to see him looking at her as though he had never seen her before. Suddenly there was hope.

She wanted to run to him, but she resisted the temptation and glided gently to his side, smiling with a gentle inner triumph.

The Vicar cleared his throat and began,

"*Dearly beloved, we are gathered here to join together this man and this woman –* "

She had never seen Robin look so handsome. He was grave and solemn as he took her hand, saying,

"*I, Robin, take thee Celina, to my wedded wife –* "

She clung to every word, especially, "*to love and to cherish.*"

She would make it happen, she promised herself.

She made her responses in a clear voice that she tried to keep steady, but she could not prevent a slight tremble as she intoned, "*to love, cherish and to obey.*"

Then came the moment when he slid the ring onto her finger, saying,

"*With this ring I thee wed. With my body I thee worship –* "

Then it was over. The Vicar smiled and said,

"You may kiss the bride."

Robin was smiling as he raised her chin with his fingers and laid his lips softly on hers.

At once a violent, almost uncontrollable tremor shook her. Unlike the fierce kiss he had given her earlier, his mouth was barely touching hers. And yet the feelings that coursed through her were even more intense than on that wonderful occasion.

Every inch of her was alive to him, longing for his touch. It was the most shattering sensation of her life, and when he released her she was gazing at him in amazement.

She thought she caught a glimpse of a new expression in his eyes, as though he too had been taken aback. But then it vanished and she could not be sure.

Next they were walking back down the aisle to where the Chapel door led out into the hall. From here it was a short step to the banqueting hall where the long tables were laid out for the guests.

Like the Chapel, this too was packed to the roof. Flowers from the gardens were placed in posies along the tables, and the best Torrington china was laid out with crystal glasses.

It was obvious that the Torrington chef and his staff had been working long hours. The towering wedding cake testified to his skills.

The bride and groom and their relatives were placed in the centre of a table raised on a dais. From here Celina could look down the room and take in the sight of the guests hurrying to find their seats.

"Is something the matter?" Robin asked her.

"No, it's just – just that I had not expected to see so many people here."

"My mother issued her commands and naturally everyone jumped to obey," he said with wry humour. "You will find that the power of a Countess is considerable." Then he added with a wicked gleam, "not as great as a Marchioness, of course."

"I think we should agree to consider that matter closed," she commented with a prim air.

He gave a broad grin which made him look more attractive than ever and she laughed with him.

Guests watching them, thought how charming it was to see a bridal couple so pleased with each other and, obviously, so much in love.

The Dowager, her eyes on them, saw their laughter and crossed her fingers.

Despite the strangeness of the arrangements the wedding feast was very much as a feast should be. Speeches were made, although they were shorter than was normal and contained no jokes.

Robin, who prided himself on being master of every situation, made an elegant speech in which he complimented his bride, but saved his greatest praise for his mother.

"She has been the finest mother a man could ever have," he said. "She has run the estate for me when I was unable to be present – "

There was a slight stir in the banqueting hall. Of all those seated at the gorgeous tables there were few who did not know the true reason behind his absences.

But Robin ignored the murmur and continued,

"Everyone who knows her, loves her, and I ask you to raise your glasses to her now."

Everyone did so, including the new young Countess, who gave her mother-in-law a special smile and received one in return.

Overwhelmed by love and gratitude she rose to her feet and ran to the Dowager, passing behind Robin's chair.

The old Dowager reached up and drew the bride's head down to plant a kiss on her cheek.

"I knew I was right," she whispered. "We did it, didn't we?"

Celina was not quite certain what these last words meant. So she merely smiled and said,

"Yes, indeed we did."

As she returned to her seat she was aware of Robin eyeing her curiously, but before he could speak the band began to play and it was time for the new husband and wife to dance together.

With an elegant gesture he took her hand and led her onto the floor. Then his arm was about her waist and the groom was swirling the bride around the floor, her dress and veil flaring out so that she seemed to be enveloped in a magic cloud.

"My congratulations," he said. "You have contrived to look magnificent. You do me credit."

She would have preferred something a little more romantic, but she cherished the compliment, smiling up into his face and saying,

"Every bride hopes to hear her groom say such lovely words."

"Of course, we are not exactly like most brides and grooms," he observed.

"I should hope not. How boring to be just like the others!"

"You speak the truth!"

"And now I come to think of it, I don't believe I have ever known a time when you were just like other men."

He grinned.

"You may find that I am even more original than you give me credit for, ma'am."

She gave a teasing laugh.

"I look forward to it."

He held her closer.

"So do I, ma'am. I promise you, so do I."

His words sent her into a daze of delight, for they seemed to hold much promise for the night to come.

If only, she thought, all these people would go home and leave them alone together. Then he would come to her and make her truly his wife. Heated tremors of anticipation coursed through her body.

Meeting his eyes, she saw that he was regarding her intently and she wondered if he had sensed what was happening to her.

She knew that if he had she ought to be ashamed, for a virtuous bride was supposed to know nothing of passion until her husband taught her.

But she could not help herself. Desire for him ran through her like liquid fire, reaching down to her toes and out to her fingertips. Who cared if he knew? She *wanted* him to know.

He seemed to be speaking to her from a great distance.

"I wish the night was here already."

Had he really said that, or was it only the echo of her own fevered thoughts?

"Yes – " she gasped.

"Do you wish that too?"

"Yes – yes – I can hardly breathe – you are holding me so tightly."

"Don't you want me to hold you?"

"*Yes* – " she said wildly.

"Then tonight I will hold you tighter still. I shall make you mine and you will belong to me forever. Do you understand me?"

She could only nod. All the strength seemed to have drained out of her and it was only his arms that were holding her up.

She felt him draw her closer yet, until his lips were touching hers and she was helpless to do anything but yield to his kiss.

She emerged from her daze to hear the incredible sound of applause. Looking round she saw that the other dancers were gathered about them, cheering at the sight of such a happy couple.

"I think we should leave the floor," he murmured. "I don't much like making an exhibition of myself."

He was right, she thought. Such joys were for later, when they were alone.

He led her off the floor, waved away another man who would have invited her to dance, bowed and left her.

She was glad to be alone for a moment to get her breath back and recover her thoughts.

In a few dazzling minutes the whole world had changed.

She had noticed the brusque gesture with which Robin had discouraged the man who wanted to dance with her and it dawned on her, like a flash of lightning, that he was jealous.

How wonderful! she thought. For so long she had felt jealous of every other woman in his life. And now he was jealous – of *her!*

She wanted to sing aloud that the world was a wonderful place and she was the happiest of mortals.

She suddenly noticed that the doctor, who was among the guests, was looking at the Dowager worriedly.

"I think you should not stay here much longer," he said to her in a low voice. "I understand that you wanted to witness the wedding, but you should now go to bed."

"Very well," the Dowager agreed reluctantly. "I am enjoying myself, but perhaps I should go. I still have duties that must be done." She looked at Celina fondly. "One duty, especially."

"Shall I fetch his Lordship?" the doctor asked, glancing to a corner where Robin was now laughing with some male friends.

"No, I don't want to worry him," the Dowager said. "Celina, my dear, come with me. There are things I want to show you."

At the bottom of the stairs she pulled herself out of her wheelchair, insisting that she could manage for herself and climbed up slowly but firmly.

"This way," she said, indicating the bedroom that had always been hers.

Celina followed her in, expecting to help put her to bed, but she stopped on the threshold, stunned by the room's transformation. New curtains were on the windows, new drapes hung around the four poster bed and everywhere there were flowers.

"This is your room now," the Dowager announced.

"But – no – I cannot drive you from your room," Celina stammered.

"This room is always occupied by the Countess of Torrington and that is now you. I remain the Dowager Countess and very happy to be so."

Celina understood. A connecting door led from this room to Robin's. Her mother-in-law had set her heart on a grandchild.

And it was only right and natural that she and Robin should be so close.

Tonight was their wedding night when he would come to her and take her in his arms.

Then the passion that she had felt flare up at his kiss would be fulfilled, and they would be truly united as man and wife.

At the thought, she felt a thrilling warmth surge through her body, as though she was blushing all over.

"Champagne!" the Dowager cried. "I wish to drink champagne with my beloved daughter-in-law."

A servant hurried away and returned with champagne.

The Dowager was next showing Celina around the room that was now hers with its huge magnificent bed hung with silk, the antique furniture, the little room attached where her maid would sleep.

Everything was magnificent, a tribute to the rank and pride of the Dowager Countess, the most socially important lady in the district.

But that was herself, she now realised. Her mother-in-law had retired into the secondary role of a dowager, glad to do so since she was realising her wish and she, Celina, now reigned supreme.

Nobody could doubt that the Dowager was pleased. There was real joy in her eyes as she toasted the new Lady Torrington and when they had clinked glasses she gave a little twirl of delight.

"Careful," Celina said anxiously. "Remember that you are still unwell. You must conserve your strength."

"My dear, I am feeling better every minute. Suddenly I have a new lease of life. Thank you, thank you."

Delighted for her, Celina took her hand and smiled.

There was a sudden silence.

Looking up, Celina saw Robin standing in the doorway.

Behind him, in the corridor just outside the room were a small crowd of laughing friends. They all looked brilliantly happy as guests at a wedding ought to look.

Only Robin did not seem to glow with happiness. He was regarding them with a strange expression on his face.

It was cold and reserved and filled Celina with a sudden fear.

"My dear boy!" the Dowager called with pleasure, turning to him with her arms outstretched. "Join us in a glass of champagne."

"Thank you, I will."

His manner was impeccable. He accepted a glass and raised it to his mother, but his eyes were stony.

"I am glad to see you are so much improved, Mama. It is delightful – and unexpected."

"Such a happy occasion," his mother sighed, "it has affected me like a tonic. If only you knew how much better I feel."

"I think I do know," he said slowly. "Yes, many things are now becoming clear to me."

He had moved towards his mother and Celina and now spoke in a low voice, so that only they could hear.

It seemed that the Dowager had also sensed something was wrong. Slowly she raised her glass to her son and spoke in a slightly nervous voice.

"I wish you both long life and happiness," she proposed.

"An excellent toast," he agreed. "Happiness – and long life."

It was at that moment that the first icy trickles of fear began to trouble Celina. She tried to ignore them. The suspicion growing inside her was surely impossible?

But there was a cold glint in Robins eyes, barely disguising an even colder rage.

She told herself that it was only her imagination. This was her wedding day and until now everything had been going so well.

'Please,' she prayed, 'do not let anything go wrong now.'

But she would not allow these fears to appear in her face. This was the day she had dreamed of for years, the day she married the man she adored and nothing must spoil it.

"*Happiness and long life*," she agreed, raising her

72

glass and meeting his gaze steadily.

For a moment it almost seemed as though he was disconcerted, unsure of himself. Then his expression hardened again.

"Shall we return to our guests?" he asked smoothly. "This is – after all – a wedding." He gave a frozen smile. "The happiest day of my life. *Let us celebrate!*"

The last words were a cry, though whether of delight or rage it was impossible to say. But Celina thought she knew.

He led the way out of the room, apparently the picture of the happy bridegroom.

"Let us all go down," the Dowager said. "I want to dance."

"Is that wise in your state of health?" Celina asked.

"Oh, my dear, a little dance will not hurt me. Besides, I may have exaggerated my illness a little, but does that really matter?"

"Matter?" she echoed, aghast. "You told Robin you were dying."

"I even managed to fool the doctor," the Dowager admitted with a smile of pleasure at her own cleverness.

"But you used it to bring about this marriage," Celina said in a horrified whisper.

"Of course I did. I had to do something or the situation would have dragged on for ever. It was high time Robin married."

"You deceived us," Celina cried.

"Well, yes, that was a pity but do you really mind, my dear? I have always believed that you felt a tenderness for Robin. Did you really not want to marry him?"

"Not like this. Never like this."

"As long as the right people are married, it doesn't

matter how," her mother-in-law said wisely.

"But it does," Celina said, almost in tears.

"Things will work out in the end. I know Robin is very fond of you, and he will be so overjoyed that I am now well after all that he will forgive us."

"Us?"

"Very well, me. It will be all right. Don't worry."

But would it be all right? Celina felt the gravest doubts. She had seen the rage in her new husband's eyes and she knew what it meant. He had seen and understood.

Suddenly everything was bathed in a horrid light.

The joy she had felt only a few moments ago had vanished. It had all been a terrible illusion and now there was a price to be paid.

But first she must endure the rest of the celebrations, smiling and looking as though she had not a care in the world.

She followed the Dowager downstairs to where she could hear music playing and the dancers were still twirling around the floor.

After a moment she could see Robin dancing with a young girl, spinning madly in time to the music. As the waltz ended he turned towards another girl and held out his hands.

One by one, he danced with every pretty girl in the room, and the onlookers murmured their approval of the groom who paid attention to so many guests when he must secretly long to be alone with his wife.

Only Celina understood that he was avoiding her.

Once, as she was dancing with the Mayor, she caught sight of Robin's face, close to her. His eyes were dark with anger. Then the turn of the dance took him away.

At last the wedding party was over. The carriages

lined up at the door and the guests trooped out to climb into them and depart.

"I shall retire now," the Dowager said. "It has been a long day and it has left me wearied."

"Let me come with you ma'am," Celina offered.

"Goodnight Mama," Robin said and kissed his mother on the cheek.

From the garden came a burst of male laughter. Some of the guests had lingered.

"I must go and see how long they intend to remain," Robin said and departed, after giving a little bow to his mother and his wife.

The doctor also came upstairs and fussed about the Dowager, taking her temperature and listening to her breathing until he was quite satisfied.

He too, Celina realised, had been completely fooled about her condition. How brilliantly she had played her part, so that nobody suspected.

When everyone else had left, Celina stood at the window, looking out onto the garden, where the darkness was broken by only a few lamps.

Suddenly there was another roar of laughter from a place under the trees.

Celina could not see too well, but she just managed to make out a rustic table, around which several men were sitting, with beer tankards in their hands.

One of them was Robin.

He was clearly enjoying himself, exchanging jokes with his friends and quaffing from his tankard. He looked like a man who meant to stay there for a long time.

'He is just being polite,' she reassured herself.

"Come and bid me goodnight," the Dowager called from her bed.

She held out her arms and Celina bent down, kissing her with affection.

"Now hurry to your room and make yourself ready for him," she said. "He is probably in his own room at this very minute, pacing the floor, impatient for his wedding night. You must not keep an eager bridegroom waiting."

"No ma'am."

This was not the moment to confide her fears.

Nora, her new maid was waiting for her. She helped Celina out of her wedding dress and into the gorgeous nightdress in which she would await her groom.

Then Celina sat at the dressing table while the maid brushed her long hair until it cascaded over her shoulders, almost down to her waist.

Soon he would be here, wreathing his hands through her hair, burying his face in it before raising his eyes to her face.

But what would she see in those eyes?

"Goodnight," Nora said at last, adding, "my Lady."

My Lady. It was true. She was Lady Torrington, the Countess, the Earl's bride.

But it all held a false and hollow ring. He was not pacing up and down, eager to come to his bride and consummate their love.

She turned out the lamp and walked again quickly to the window overlooking the garden. From here she could see the place where he had been sitting. Some of the men were still there.

But he had vanished.

Where was he? What would he do now?

She stood there, in the darkness of the silent house, waiting and wondering, her heart beating urgently with anticipation.

CHAPTER SIX

At last Celina heard a footstep in Robin's room next door. She held her breath.

How long now? A few minutes to undress, then he would come to her in his dressing gown. And then –

Her heartbeat quickened.

But it was only a few seconds later that she heard a sound from the door. She watched as the handle turned, very slowly and quietly. The door swung open and there he was on the threshold.

He was still fully dressed and he stood there, regarding her in her glorious lacy nightwear. She turned so that he could see her better, but no pleasure came into his eyes.

In fact, something about him made her wonder if he was slightly the worse for wear.

"You are still awake?" he asked coolly.

"But of course I am. I have been waiting for you."

"Like a devoted wife," he observed ironically and it was almost a sneer.

She flinched at the sound, but tried to reply calmly,

"That is what I intend to be."

He began to laugh, not in a friendly way, but like a man enjoying a bitter joke.

"I am sure your intentions are of the best, my dear."

"I don't – quite know what you mean by that."

"Don't you? I would have thought you probably did, but we will leave it for the moment."

He advanced further into the room and she became even more certain that he had taken a little too much to drink.

Her heart sank.

"Did your wedding live up to your expectations, madam?" he enquired sardonically.

"My wedding? Surely it was *our* wedding?"

"Was it? I must admit that I had a slightly uninvolved feeling, as though I was only there as the sacrifice being led to the slaughter."

"What a strange thing to say."

"The point about the sacrifice is that nobody tells the poor fool anything. They dress him up, lead him to the altar and just when he thinks he is the centre of a big celebration, he finds himself facing the High Priestesses sharpening their knives. It is certainly an interesting feeling."

"And just who do you think are the High Priestesses?" she asked, beginning to become angry in her turn.

He shrugged.

"I think we both know who they are."

"Both?" she repeated, horrified. "Are you suggesting that I connived to force you into this marriage?"

"Let's not be squeamish about it. The trick worked. I did not find out until it was too late, did I? I congratulate you."

"How dare you!" she screamed. "How dare you suggest that I plotted all this!"

He came to stand directly in front of her, regarding her with a bitterness that made her heart thump with dread.

"My mother isn't dying at all, is she?"

"I – "

"Is she?"

"How do you expect me to know?" she cried.

How cold his eyes were! As cold as hate as he said,

"If you do not give me a straight answer – "

"All right, she is not dying. She told me that today."

"Oh, I think she told you a lot earlier than that."

"I swear that she did not – "

"I saw you with your heads together at the reception, chuckling over the way your little conspiracy had worked out so well."

"No, that wasn't – "

"You knew exactly what was really happening before I even came home, didn't you?"

"No – "

"Don't deny it. It was a plot to entice me back here, tied up in wedding ribbons and delivered into marital bondage."

He turned away and began to stride about the room.

She watched him, filled with misery at the ruin of her wedding night. She could not blame him for being angry about his mother's plot, but that he should think herself part of it was unbearable. After the years they had known each other, he should have trusted her more.

At this moment she almost detested him.

"I knew nothing about it until tonight. You must believe me."

"But I do not believe you. I saw the two of you congratulating each other on a job well done."

"That is just not true," she cried. "I was horrified when I found out. I told her it was the wrong way to go about things but it was too late by then."

"I still do not believe you."

"I am not a liar," she asserted hotly.

"So you say. But how can I believe any words of yours. If my mother could deceive me, so could you.

"And now I come to think of it, the deceit was very cleverly done. Your refusal of a proposal that I had not made, the letter to my mother that brought me to you, determined to change your mind. What a clever trap and how easily I fell into it."

"Are you daring to suggest that I wrote that letter on purpose? It was meant only for your mother's eyes."

"But you knew I would see it, didn't you?"

That much was certainly true, but not for the reason he thought. Horrified, she turned away, pressing her hands to her cheeks to hide her sudden blushes.

"Do not turn away from me," he snapped, pulling her round to face him. "It is time we had a talk."

"What's the point?" she cried. "You only want to hear what suits you."

"And you will only say what suits you," he sneered. "You are right. There is no point in talking. The deed is done and it is too late to undo it now."

"But it isn't," she answered with spirit. "If you feel you were tricked into marriage, then clearly we must seek an immediate annulment."

He whirled on her and she flinched away from the murder in his eyes.

"Annulment?" he raged in a soft, venomous voice. "Are you insane to suggest such an idea? Do you think I am going to reveal to the world that I was tricked by a pair of women? Shall I make myself a buffoon for the neighbourhood to laugh at? If you think that, you much misunderstand me, madam."

"I don't – "

"Listen to me," he said fiercely. "I said that what is done is done. We are married and we will have to stay married, however painful such a marriage will be for both of us."

"But why does it have to be painful?" she cried.

"Because I will not allow you to gloat over me, madam. You will find the fruits of your 'victory' will turn to ashes."

She could not bear this torture a moment longer. The fury in his eyes seemed to tear into her and she turned aside, desperate to run away from him.

But he seized her, his hands on both shoulders.

"Stay here and listen to me," he hissed through gritted teeth.

"I don't want to hear anything you have to say while you are like this," she screamed. "For pity's sake leave it until tomorrow, when we will both be calmer and – "

"Calmer? I shall never be calm again. Outside, I shall observe all the husbandly proprieties, but inside me there will be a hatred that you will never understand."

"Then let us end it with an annulment," she repeated bitterly.

"I have told you, *no*. You have made your bed and now you must lie on it – an apt phrase, since this is our wedding night."

She read the intention in his eyes and tried to pull away in horror but his hands were hurting her shoulders.

"Let me go," she gasped.

"And deprive you of your victory? This is your moment of success, when I will truly become your husband and no power on earth can separate us again."

He pulled her close and the next moment his lips were forced onto hers, fierce, crushing, cruel.

She had dreamed of this moment, when he would embrace her in the first kiss of their married life, then carry her to bed for the flowering of passion.

But now the moment was here, she was in his arms while he smothered her with kisses and all she could feel was anger and revulsion.

Never in her wildest dreams had she thought that her husband would make love to her with loathing and contempt.

Now it was happening and she could not bear it.

"No," she howled frantically. "Not like this."

She tried to push him away, but there was a burning light in his eyes that she had never seen before. Suddenly he was a stranger.

"You are my wife, madam," he said harshly. "This is no time to be coy."

"I am not your wife," she responded in a hoarse whisper. "Nor shall I ever be. You are not the only one who can hate."

She could barely say the last word. His lips were on hers again, silencing her cries, while his arms held her in a merciless grip.

If only the moment had been different, this would be divinely wonderful. Even now she could feel the thrill in her blood at his nearness, the hot, masculine smell of him with its promise of passion.

But this was not passion. He was embracing her with scorn and if she did not fight him they would both regret it all their days. Whatever happened between them, it must not be like this.

In a last desperate struggle she managed to wrench herself free of him. But he was not to be deterred. She saw him reach for her again, and in that split second she drew back her hand and slapped him across the face with all her strength.

The shock checked him. He stood regarding her, breathing hard.

"Don't come any nearer!" she cried. "I mean it."

His mouth twisted into a bitter grin.

"A little melodramatic, madam," he grated. "A man is expected to make love to his bride."

"Not when he has just insulted her. You think that I am so grateful to bear your name that I will settle for any treatment? You will discover that you are wrong."

She took a deep breath.

"Now, I would like you to leave."

He gave a crackle of laughter.

"You cannot be serious."

"I am completely serious. This is my room and I wish to retire for the night. Kindly leave."

She spoke with all the chilly dignity that she could muster, but inwardly she was trembling. She could not force him to leave and if he defied her, she was helpless.

He was staring at her.

"You are serious?"

"Completely serious."

"By Heaven, you have the cheek of the devil."

"No, sir, I am not the devil, merely a woman who will not allow herself to be abused."

"*You are my wife!*"

It took all her courage to say quietly,

"No, I am not. Nor do I ever wish to be."

His eyes narrowed and for a dreadful moment she thought that he was going to force the issue. But then he shrugged and gave a sharp angry grunt.

"This matter is not over, madam."

"Goodnight, sir."

He turned and walked away through the door that connected their rooms. At once she ran after him and turned the key in the lock, before hurrying to secure the outer door as well.

Only when she felt safe did she throw herself onto her bed and sob her heart out.

This was her wedding night.

*

Celina had expected to lie awake all night, but she was finally overcome with exhaustion and sank into a deep sleep. At dawn she awoke and lay for a moment wondering where she was.

Then she remembered.

She wanted to weep again with despair at the crushing of her dream, but she refused to yield to weakness. She could not spend her life in weeping.

She became aware that someone was knocking at her door and hurried over. But she did not open it.

"Who is it?" she asked cautiously.

"Nora, my Lady," came a soft voice.

Celina opened the door and found the maid outside, looking anxious.

"Shall I bring your Ladyship some tea?" she asked.

"Thank you, I should like some tea."

"Then your dresser will come to help you select what you wish to wear today."

"My dresser?"

"Mrs. Ragley."

"But is she not Lady Torrington's dresser?"

Nora looked at her as though she was mad.

"But *you* are Lady Torrington," she declared.

"Oh, yes, so I am."

It seemed that, as a Countess, she could not make do with a mere maid. Only a dresser would do.

From then on Celina felt as though she had been caught up in a machine that dealt with her in stages and passed her on to the next section.

Her tea arrived, followed by two under-maids, bearing jugs of hot water which they poured into a hip bath and then returned to the kitchen for more.

When Nora was satisfied that the bath water was perfect, she stood aside and indicated that Celina should get in. She did so and was thoroughly sponged by her efficient maid.

Only when she had been dried off did Mrs. Ragley appear to pronounce on Celina's clothes, such as they were. They had been sent over from her house the day before the wedding and Celina guessed that the awesome dresser had already inspected them thoroughly.

"Has your Ladyship decided how to spend today?" she enquired.

Lost in her strange situation, Celina had made no plans and said the first thing that came into her head.

"I think I should like to go riding."

Mrs. Ragley took her riding dress from the wardrobe and laid it out. She spoke not a word, but she managed to convey her view that the garment was a temporary affair, soon to be replaced with one more suitable for the Countess of Torrington.

But even she gave a brief nod of satisfaction at the sight of the new Countess in the dark green costume that emphasised her excellent shape, especially her tiny waist. She curtsied and left the room.

Breakfast would be waiting for her in the morning room, downstairs. But where was Robin?

Then she glanced out of the window and saw him riding under the trees. There was no other possible course. She must go down and face him.

To her relief the morning room was empty, except for Crale, the butler, waiting to serve her from the luxurious spread set out on long tables. Celina had been afraid that the Dowager might be there and she would not have known what to say to her.

A major battle was approaching, even bigger than the duel of the previous night. She was going to need all her strength to stand up to him.

'And stand up to him is something I simply must do,' she told herself. 'Otherwise there is no hope.'

But hope for what, she wondered.

Hope for his love? For a happy marriage?

They were impossible now. The best that might be secured was a conflict of equals, in which neither yielded but neither gained.

It was a bleak prospect.

At last she saw his shadow outside the tall French windows that opened onto the terrace and the next moment he had entered the morning room.

"Good morning, madam," he said, speaking with cool propriety in front of the butler.

She returned his greeting in the same manner and waited while he accepted a cup of coffee, before indicating to Crale to depart. With a low bow, he closed the doors behind him.

Silence. Each was waiting for the other to speak.

Celina gave him a brief glance. Very faintly on his face she could see the mark that her hand had left last night and it shocked her to realise how hard she must have struck him.

She looked away, but not before he had seen her glance and thought that he understood it.

"Relishing your victory, madam?" he asked in a cold voice that was almost a sneer.

"Not at all," she replied, determined to remain calm. "I do not regard it as a victory."

"Very wise of you, for matters cannot be allowed to remain as they are."

"I agree. The sooner we put matters to rights the better."

"And your idea of putting matters right is – ?"

"I told you last night. We must separate and untie the knot as soon as possible."

"And I told you that it's impossible."

"Why should it be? Neither of us likes the other or wants remain married. Do you think I want to be your wife after the way you have accused and insulted me?"

"I had some reason for my suspicions, I think."

"You had none. Your mother deceived me as she deceived you and if you had thought about it for a moment you would have realised that."

"It just seemed a little too much of a coincidence. I have been the prey of scheming females for years."

Celina turned on him.

"So that means I am a scheming female? Your conceit is beyond all bounds. I planned the whole escapade, did I? No doubt I also arranged for Lord Delaine to propose to me in London and pursue me when I refused him. Then you walked into my home and found him seizing me in his arms, forcing his ring on my finger. How brilliant I must be to have planned all that!"

She waited to see if he could answer her barrage, but he remained silent, watching her through narrowed eyes.

"And just why do you suggest I did it?" she resumed.

She had managed to overcome her anger and assumed an air of amusement.

"Was I anxious to marry for a great title? If so, why did I not marry Lord Delaine, whose title is greater than yours? Why would any woman settle for a mere Earl when she could wed a Marquis?"

"That would depend on the Marquis," he growled. "I doubt if even Delaine's title could make him acceptable to a woman of sensibility."

"So now I am a woman of sensibility?" she asked with a touch of mockery. "Last night, according to you, I was a scheming harpy, so desperate to marry that I would conspire to trap you. The accusation is preposterous, but you have never minded talking nonsense."

"Delaine is a fool," he snapped.

"Yes, he is a fool. But he is a kindly man and he adores me. A woman could be very happy with a husband like him. Choose you over him? You must have windmills in your head."

"And yet you did choose me over him."

"For the sake of your mother, whom I believed to be dying. I too was deceived. Had I known the truth, nothing on earth could have prevailed on me to make such a sacrifice."

"Be careful, madam. You will go too far."

Her blood was up and she faced him with reckless courage.

"Too far?" she echoed defiantly. "In our present situation, my Lord, what exactly would you define as too far?"

He drew breath to reply but, with perfect timing, she interrupted, saying,

"Never mind. I shall speak as I please."

"You always have, as I recall. I had forgotten what a sharp-tongued witch you can be."

"And now that you have remembered, you will be as glad to be rid of me as I will be of you."

"That is impossible."

"Nothing is impossible if you really want it and I am very sure that we both desire an end to this mockery of a marriage."

"Do we? As I said last night, I am not eager to expose myself to the County's derision by splitting from my wife the morning after our wedding. Are you? Have you thought about how it will look if you drive back home now?

"What will people say about you, Celina? That you were rejected by your husband. You can tell them the truth until kingdom come, but nobody will believe you. Some of them will laugh at you, some will pity you, but nobody will ever take you seriously again."

It was all true, she realised. Surely anything was better than being an object of scorn in the district for the rest of her life?

Robin heard his own words with astonishment. This was not what he had meant to say to her. He had come with the fixed intention of telling her to forget her foolish ideas about an annulment, because he had decided otherwise. If she protested he would inform her that he was the master and she would obey him.

Instead he was arguing with her, actually trying to persuade her, as though her opinion mattered.

Worst of all, he actually found himself saying,

"I suggest you think it over before coming to a hasty decision."

"Or having a decision forced on me," she threw at him.

He had the grace to redden, which made the mark on his face even more noticeable.

His voice became stiff and formal.

"Let me assure you, madam, that there will be no repetition of that unfortunate incident."

She faced him.

"There had better not be," she said quietly. "Because if there is, I shall leave at once and you can tell the world whatever you please."

It was safe to say that nobody had spoken to his Lordship in such a way since he became a man.

But he checked the furious response that rose to his lips. He was caught and he knew it, because he feared derision and she, apparently, did not.

What could a man do with such a woman? How could he control her?

He couldn't. That was the answer.

And a wise man would admit it now, cut his losses and be rid of her.

But even as he pondered the idea, the thought came to him that this was a woman like no other, and that their battle would be more interesting than any encounter with the easy ladies who cost him so much and bored him so easily.

"You have my word as a gentleman, madam. But do not take too long in making up your mind."

"I shall take as long as I need. You have, after all, given your word."

"Certainly, but – "

"If you intend to break your word, it would be the shortest promise on record, even for you."

"May I ask what you mean by that?"

"Come, come, your habits are well known. Don't be so modest."

"If you mean what I think you do, then this is a most improper conversation," he said furiously.

"You are right, talking is a waste of time," she stated with a calm that was calculated to infuriate him. "I intend to go for a ride, if you do have a suitable horse in your stables."

"I doubt that you will have any fault to find with my horses," he responded stiffly.

"Exactly. They are *your* horses. I don't suppose there is one suitable for me."

"I shall escort you out to the stables and prove you wrong. Shall we go, madam?"

"Certainly, my Lord."

In the stables he introduced her to Frank, a stocky middle-aged man whom, he informed her, would be her personal groom.

"Her Ladyship needs a horse to ride."

"Just as I thought," Frank said gleefully. "I have two for her Ladyship's inspection."

"Only two?" Robin demanded. "That's rather meagre for the Torrington stables."

"But there has been so little demand for a lady's riding horse," Frank explained. "Your esteemed Mama only uses the carriage."

"True. Well, let's have a look at what you have."

The two animals in question were excellent beasts in their way but undistinguished. Celina chose one for the day's ride, but Robin looked displeased.

"That will do for the moment, but something better must be found. In the meantime, Frank, saddle this animal and accompany her Ladyship on her ride."

He gave a brief bow to his wife and departed, trying not to see the astonishment on the faces of the stable staff that the newly-weds were not going to ride out together.

Celina saw them too, but was determined to ignore them and enjoy her ride. Frank was a pleasant companion who willingly took her to far-flung parts of the estate that she had not seen before.

But she wanted a really good energetic ride and at last she urged her steed forward into a gallop, forcing Frank to race after her.

Scenery raced by her, and she became exhilarated by the joy of speed. Frank only just managed to keep up.

"Oh, that was so good," she enthused at last.

Her voice faded as she caught sight of something that made her frown.

"Who are those people?" she asked.

Frank followed her glance to where two men stood watching them. They were shabby and unshaven and there was something unnerving about their unflinching gaze.

"Come away, my Lady," Frank urged her hurriedly.

"But who are they?"

"Nobody."

"But they must be somebody."

"Estate workers. Nobody who matters."

"But of course they matter. They don't look happy."

"They're scowling because they're malcontents, always complaining about something. Lord Torrington would be most displeased if he knew you had encountered such persons. They are far beneath you."

Plainly the man was afraid of getting into trouble so Celina said no more and allowed him to escort her home. But she silently resolved to return to this spot one day soon and explore further.

CHAPTER SEVEN

When they reached the castle, Frank escorted Celina right to the front door, helped her dismount and then took both horses off to the stables.

As soon as she had climbed the steps, she saw her mother-in-law coming to meet her, arms outstretched.

"So there you are. I have been so looking forward to greeting you this morning. I am so happy. But why did you go riding without Robin? It is his job to show you around your new home."

Suddenly Celina realised that she was caught in a trap. She had no idea whether Robin and his mother had talked or whether she knew that he had guessed the truth.

Before she could think of a cautious reply, Robin appeared in the hall behind his mother.

In answer to her querying look, he shook his head.

'So the Dowager still believed that he was deluded,' Celina thought with dismay.

"I have been occupied finding a suitable mare for my bride," he said. "I ordered her to be brought round as soon as you arrived. I think she must be here by now."

He spoke in response to the sight of Frank appearing in the front doorway. He wore a look of delight.

Together they walked out and inspected the grey mare

held by an under-groom. She had large, gentle eyes and Celina fell in love with her at once.

"How beautiful!" she exclaimed.

Frank assisted her into the saddle and she trotted around the garden. By the time she returned she knew that this was the perfect horse for her.

As he watched her ride back to the house, Robin nodded with satisfaction.

"Buy the animal," he told Frank. "Whatever the owner asks, pay it."

As the three of them strolled back into the house he said,

"Frank just admitted that he has had his eye on the mare for a while, waiting for me to marry."

"The whole estate has been waiting for you to marry," his mother added excitedly. "And now everyone is happy and looking to the future.

"Oh, Robin, it is so wonderful that this has finally happened! I am afraid I have been too ill to attend to so many things I should have done on the estate, but now you are here with the bride I have always wanted for you."

There was a pause before she continued,

"Perhaps even sooner than we expect, you will have the son I have longed and prayed for."

Celina caught Robin's eye, silently reproaching him for not having been honest with his mother.

He cleared his throat awkwardly,

"Mama," he said, leading the way into the library, "I have something to tell you."

"Oh, let me sit down, in case it is too much for me," the Dowager said, fanning her face with her hand and beginning to breathe hard.

"Mama, you can stop that now."

"He knows," Celina whispered.

The Dowager's response was a trill of laughter.

"Oh, dear, I should have thought of that. I gave myself away yesterday, didn't I? And I suppose you told him, Celina dear."

"No ma'am, he noticed for himself."

"And are you very angry with me?" she asked her son. "You won't blame me, will you? It was just an innocent little deception and it means so much to me."

For a moment Celina thought he would tell her just how angry he was, but after a moment Robin sighed and said,

"You should not have deceived me, Mama, but I dare say things will work out well in the end."

His mother regarded him with eyes that were disconcertingly shrewd.

"You are angry," she said. "I suppose I cannot blame you. But just wait and see what an excellent wife Celina will make you. And Celina, you must not be angry either, because you are going to have the most delightful time."

"Really, ma'am?" And for the life of her Celina could not keep a wry note out of her voice.

Robin heard it and grinned, but did not speak.

"You married in such a hurry that there was no time for you to acquire a trousseau, so I am going to see to it that you have a complete new wardrobe," the Dowager resumed.

"There is no need, ma'am," Celina said, thinking that she might not stay very long.

The Dowager looked grave.

"Oh, my dear, there *is* a need. There really is, believe me."

Which was as close as this courteous lady would come to saying that Celina's clothes were totally inadequate for her new position in the world.

"I will arrange a meeting this afternoon with everyone you will need to take care of you," she said.

"I am amazed that the meeting has not already been arranged," Robin observed cynically.

"Well, I may just have dropped a hint or two. Things have to be planned, you know."

"I suppose they do," he murmured.

"Just wait until you see your bride in her new clothes, with her hair dressed in a new way and glittering with the Torrington jewels. I don't suppose you have thought to give them to her yet, have you?"

"No," he said uneasily. "Everything has been so sudden."

"And a great deal remains to be done. Now, you two go away and change your clothes, and I will see you at lunch."

With his mother's keen eyes upon him Robin ceremoniously offered his arm to his bride and together they climbed the stairs.

"I am glad you like your mare," he said politely.

"She is the most beautiful creature I have ever seen," she enthused warmly. "I shall call her White Fire. I think she is perfect."

He shrugged.

"As my mother says, everything must be right for the new Lady Torrington. That is only appropriate."

He opened the door for her, revealing Nora laying out her clothes for lunch.

"I will leave you ma'am," he said formally, "and we will see each other in an hour."

The Dowager was in a merry mood at lunch. It did not seem to have occurred to her that anybody could object to her ruse.

Her only reaction to having her secret out in the open was relief that she need no longer bother playing her part.

Neither Robin nor Celina felt able to be so relaxed, but she was oblivious to their discomfort, rattling away in fine style about all the delightful events that would now occur.

"Everybody in the district wants to entertain you," she said. "They would have invited you during your engagement, only there wasn't one, so they are going to make up for lost time now."

"I gather that you have arranged our diary for some time ahead," Robin commented dryly.

"Not at all, merely just a couple of weeks," the Dowager replied airily. "After that, of course, you will wish to make your own decisions."

"How astute of you, Mama. Actually I would always rather make my own decisions, but you seem to possess a gift for settling matters on my behalf."

There was a faint edge to his voice and Celina intervened quickly.

"It is so kind of you, ma'am, to help me. I am so inexperienced."

"Indeed you are, my dear. Oh, what fun we are going to have buying you new clothes."

"I must remind you that I recently bought new clothes in London for the Season," she pointed out.

Her mother-in-law gave a pained smile.

"Last year's fashions!"

"It was just a few weeks ago," Celina remarked indignantly.

"The Countess of Torrington must always be in

advance of fashion," the Dowager observed grandly.

"Well, nobody in London thought my clothes were exactly dowdy."

"Yes, she received an offer from a Marquis," Robin put in slyly. "We must not forget that."

Celina threw him a sulphurous look.

"Hah! Delaine!" the Dowager snorted. "You did well not to accept him. He would not have added to your consequence."

"To marry a Marquis must always add to a woman's consequence," Celina responded, slightly nettled.

"Not if he's a nincompoop," the Dowager declared in a voice that settled the matter once and for all.

"I am afraid, Mama, that Celina feels she took a step down in the world when she married me," Robin added caustically.

His mother simply did not know what to make of this remark. After peering at them both suspiciously through her lorgnettes, she repeated "nonsense!" several times.

Celina refused to meet Robin's eye. She was afraid of finding a glint of wicked humour that she might not be able to resist.

Next Robin said,

"I have business to attend to. I will leave you ladies to attend to your own business."

He kissed his mother's cheek, bowed to his wife and departed.

"There, you see?" the Dowager said. "He is perfectly happy about the situation."

Celina thought she was being wildly optimistic, but realised that her mother-in-law knew nothing of the seething tension between herself and Robin.

She did not feel equal to long explanations, so she

settled down to enjoy the prospect of acquiring new clothes.

Although that might be premature, she reminded herself as she had not yet decided to stay at the castle.

But in the meantime, there was no harm in pleasing her mother-in-law.

After a delightful hour planning her wardrobe they rose and went upstairs, where her dresser and a seamstress were waiting.

Half way up the stairs Celina heard the door of the library open and saw a man emerge. She stopped, staring at him, thinking that she had never seen anyone that she disliked so much at first sight.

He was in his late forties with heavy features and a burly build that conveyed something brutal about it. When he glanced up at Celina, she observed a hardness in his eyes that dismayed her.

There was no respect in his manner and he returned her stare with a kind of arrogance, although his severe clothes suggested that he must be an employee of some kind.

"What it is, my dear?" the Dowager paused and laid a gentle hand on her arm.

"That man – "

"That is Stanley Halyard, the Steward."

"I don't like him."

"That is a little unfair since you do not know him. Still," she added with a sigh, "I admit he is a bit of a rough diamond and I do not enjoy too much of his company myself."

"But doesn't he report to you, ma'am, when Lord Torrington is away."

"Of course I have to meet him sometimes to discuss what is to be done, but I know I can leave matters to him and he keeps the estate running smoothly. Now, come along, we have work to do."

They worked late as Robin had sent a message that he was spending the evening with friends.

The Dowager sighed and said,

"I supposed it's too much to expect him to behave like a devoted husband just at first."

"Yes ma'am," Celina agreed in a voice that gave nothing away.

He had not returned when she retired to bed and she wondered whether he had done so on purpose so as to avoid another rebuff from her.

Or had he simply forgotten all about her?

She locked the connecting door between their rooms, thinking sadly how different this was from what she had longed for.

She lay awake as the hours passed and at last she heard him enter next door. He had been gone so long that she was sure he must have had too much to drink and strained her ears, expecting to hear heavy movements.

But, to her surprise, he moved with a lightness and precision that suggested sobriety.

If he had not been drinking, what then had he been doing? Playing cards?

Or had he been with another woman?

Was he so angry with her for refusing him that he had sought revenge in this way?

She waited to see if he would try the door, but the handle remained undisturbed.

Celina buried her face in her pillow and wept.

*

The next morning Robin greeted her with a cool civility in which she was sure she detected a hint of irony. It fired her spirit and she nodded and smiled with equal coolness.

"I hope you slept well, madam."

"Thank you, I had a very quiet night's sleep. I hope the same is true of you."

"I was out late, as I dare say you know."

"No, how could I? I was asleep before you returned – whenever that was."

Certainly she would not let him think that she had lain awake listening for him.

At breakfast he declared that he needed to spend some time away on matters of business. His mother said happily that he would not be missed as she and Celina had so much to accomplish.

"But be sure to be home by Friday," she said. "We are all invited for dinner at Beresford Manor. Simply everyone will be there to honour your bride and it would never do for you to be absent."

"You may be sure I will do my duty, Mama," he replied with a slight bow.

The week that followed was a whirl of activity. The Dowager had placed large orders with the local warehouses, and now those emporiums sent carriages which arrived to the castle laden down with luxurious materials of every kind.

Now Celina's maids and her dresser could get to work on an orgy of sewing – ball gowns, tea gowns, morning gowns, afternoon gowns, riding habits, the list of things to be done was endless.

From another warehouse came a vast selection of hats to be sorted through with some kept and some returned. There must be at least two hats for each dress and more shoes than Celina could count.

Yet another establishment, very discreet and only for ladies of the highest taste and deepest pockets, produced nightgowns of lace and silk filmy underwear and silk stockings.

Celina would have been in a heaven of delight if her mind had not been on Robin, wondering what he was doing now and who he might be with.

He might even have returned to France.

No, she thought with a spurt of anger. She would not let him tease and torment her like this. As soon as she saw him again she would tell him that their so-called marriage was over, whether he liked it or not.

When Thursday night arrived, Robin still had not returned home and Celina could tell that her mother-in-law was growing worried, although she tried to hide it.

Celina herself went off to bed with a cheerful smile and fell asleep wondering what the morrow would bring.

She awoke with the dawn, hearing the sounds of movement from the other side of the door.

So, she thought, he was home at last from carousing with his friends and perhaps his mistresses. Today she would inform him of her decision to leave, once and for all.

She found that it was impossible to go to sleep again, so she rose, dressing herself in one of her riding habits and crept quietly downstairs.

She slipped out of the castle by a back door which she knew led to the stables. At this early hour the place was only just coming to life, but she found one of the hands dozing in the stable of her mare, White Fire, who was never left unguarded, night or day, on Robin's orders.

"I'll fetch Frank," the hand offered, yawning and climbing sleepily to his feet.

"No, I just want to take the air alone. Saddle her for me please quietly."

"Alone?" the young man asked in dismay. "But I cannot allow your Ladyship to ride without an escort – "

"Allow? Do I need your permission?" she asked with

a touch of imperiousness. "Kindly saddle her at once and say nothing to anyone else. That is an order."

He gulped but obeyed.

The mare rubbed her nose against Celina's hand as she patted her and talked to her in a whisper.

With the sun shining on her and her mare eager to carry her as fast as possible, she rode out, moving faster and faster over the land.

Exhilarated by her speed, she had come further than ever before and was now in an area that looked unfamiliar.

However she did remember that she had been here on the first day out with Frank. And he had urgently turned her back.

Now, thinking she had perhaps gone far enough, she turned her horse.

Suddenly, to her surprise, out of the woods at the side of the field where she was riding, there appeared four men.

She thought they were perhaps workmen except they were so shabbily dressed that she was quite certain they were not employed on the estate.

As she drew nearer to them, she observed that they were all dirty and untidy and clearly very poor.

Suddenly, to her astonishment the men moved forward and two of them took hold of her reins.

"Who are you?" she asked. "What do you want?"

She tried not to be frightened, but they were effectively holding her prisoner.

"You come with us," one of them said. "We've got something to show you which will teach you that the man you've married ain't what you think him to be."

"Wait," she said, "haven't I seen you before?"

Now she recognised one of the men who had been standing here the first time she had ridden in this direction.

"You may have done," he replied. "I've seen you before and I know who you are. Why did you have to complain about us? We never hurt you."

"Complain? I never complained."

"They said you did. Someone came to the village later that day and said we should keep out of her Ladyship's way, because we'd upset her."

"But I never said I was upset. Never. You must believe me."

"Maybe we does and maybe we doesn't," he growled.

"Please, let me go."

But they did not move. There was nothing she could do as two of them were holding on to the reins of her mare, while the other two had placed themselves on either side of her.

They passed through a gap in the hedge and in front of her she saw several small cottages and a number of women and children watching her approach.

One glance at them told Celina they were extremely poorly dressed in clothes which were both dirty and torn. The children were thin and emaciated.

As she came to a standstill, a number of women came out from some very decrepit and unpleasant looking cottages, which had broken windows and roofs which were lacking tiles.

More women and children appeared from the cottages to stare at her. Not only were they dirty but on some of them their clothes were almost falling apart.

These were neglected, destitute people, she realised. They lived with despair.

But what were they doing on the Torrington estate?

Then one of the men holding her horse said,

"Now you'll see how we're being treated, how the

children are being starved to death. Is that what you want – that we should all die?"

Celina stared at him and did not know what to say. He was looking at her with an expression that might almost have been hatred.

"What has happened?" she asked. "Why are you in such a state?"

"She wants to know why we are like this," the man repeated ironically. "We're like this because we've no money, because no one's paid us and we're starving."

"I don't understand," Celina stammered.

"Well you married our Master and you might as well know what he's like," the man answered.

"He don't worry about us," another man said. "He just stays abroad, enjoying himself."

Celina drew in her breath.

'Can this really be true?' she asked herself.

Then she remembered that he was quite right in saying that Robin was always away.

Because he had spent so much time in France the people on his estate were suffering.

The men were still looking at her in an alarming way, but she knew that she must suppress her fear and do something positive.

The man who had neglected them was her husband and she must put matters right.

She had no idea how to do so, but never in her life had she flinched from responsibility. Now she felt a pang of guilt. She was their only hope and she too had nearly abandoned them.

To give herself time to think, she dismounted and walked to where she could see some women, who had come out from the dirty cottages. They were dreadfully thin and moved slowly, as if movement was an effort.

"Tell me what has happened," she cried.

Another man, younger than the rest, placed himself before her.

"Isn't it obvious?" he asked.

"What is your name?" she asked.

"Never mind my name. None of us here have names – not really. We're just ants to them in the castle."

"Nonetheless, I would like to know your name. I do not regard you as an ant. Please believe me."

He did not reply and she thought she understood. He was afraid of repercussions.

"Trust me," she said. "I only want to help you."

More silence.

They exchanged glances uncertainly. None of them knew what to think or say.

At last the young man admitted reluctantly,

"My name is Egan Janner."

"Thank you."

To defuse the tension she turned away and walked towards one of the seats in front of the cottages. She sat down and said,

"Now tell me what has happened and why you have no money?"

"Because his Lordship is never here," Janner replied. "He's always having fun in France and he only came back to marry you. Perhaps now you'll tell him what's been going on."

"Yes, I will tell him," Celina promised. "But why have you not been paid for your work, and why have your houses been allowed to fall into such a terrible state of disrepair?"

"I'll tell yer right enough," the man replied. "It's

because the Steward drinks away every penny he has, that's if His Lordship gives him any."

"The Steward? You mean Stanley Halyard?"

"Aye, that's him. You know him then?"

"No, I have only seen him from a distance. I didn't like the look of him."

This brought a jeering laugh from those around her.

"If *you* don't like him, how do you think we feel? We're at his mercy. He has a free hand here. He does as he likes and us gets nothing."

"I am sure if his Lordship knew what was happening he would be horrified," Celina said. "Don't worry. I will tell him."

She felt half faint with what she was hearing. How could this have happened on Robin's estate? It was easy to say that he was away and did not know, but he should have known.

Mr. Halyard was to blame, but Robin was also to blame for allowing him to get away with it.

"Now tell me more," she said. "I want to be quite certain that I know everything before I talk to my husband."

"Do you think he'll listen?" Janner asked.

"He will have to listen," Celina replied.

Two men, who had been standing back, now came forward. Celina realised they had been biting on pieces of wood.

She remembered reading once that people who were starving often ate wood because it made them think in some odd way that they were having something to eat.

Then one of the men said,

"We did what were asked of us and do you think we were paid? No. Do you know what this means to our women and children?"

"I can see it's terrible," Celina said. "And I will make sure that something is done."

"But will he do anything just because you say so?"

"I am his wife," Celina answered firmly. "I will make him listen."

Nobody spoke. They merely looked at each other.

Celina guessed that they doubted her because they did not dare to let their hopes be raised.

"I promise you," she said, "things are going to change."

"But will he stay here long enough to change anything?" a woman asked. "You'll be clever if you keeps him in England when he much prefers being in France."

"Then I shall have to be very clever," she said, trying to speak lightly. "I will go back now to speak to his Lordship."

As she spoke she realised that two of the men were whispering to each other.

Then one of them, who looked more aggressive than the others, said,

"You stay with us. If he wants you, he can come and fetch you."

"But I need to – "

"You stay with us," he repeated firmly.

She looked around their faces, all of them sullen and unyielding. They were desperate and if they were pushed too far, who knew what might happen?

There was no point in arguing. She would just have to remain patient and hope that Robin would come for her urgently.

In the meantime she was a prisoner.

CHAPTER EIGHT

"Very well," Celina agreed, trying to speak calmly, "bring me some writing paper and a pencil, so that I can write to my husband."

Egan Janner went to fetch what she needed. He returned with a scrap of paper, on which Celina wrote,

'Dearest Robin,

I am with some of your workers, who have been very badly treated. Please come as quickly as you can. They are good people and need your help.

It is most important that you come by yourself. Do not send your Steward instead or allow him to accompany you.

Your wife,

Celina.'

"I'll take it," said Janner. "I can ride your horse."

She watched as he galloped away on White Fire. Then she turned and found the others looking at her with a combination of aggression and confusion.

For a moment she was afraid. Would Robin do as she wished?

But he must, she told herself. *He must.*

"Now," she said, turning back to the women, "while we are waiting, I want to hear everything you have to tell me."

Suddenly there was a scream from one of the cottages and the next moment a woman came running out, carrying a baby in her arms.

"He's dead!" she cried. "He's dead – starved!"

She pushed the baby towards Celina, who took it into her arms, horrified at this discovery. It was tiny and obviously only a few days old. Its eyes were closed, its thin arms fell limply down beside its body and it was cold.

Yet it seemed to her that there was still a touch of life in the minute body. Very gently, while the women stared at her, she opened the little mouth.

Then she breathed gently into it, not once but three times. There was complete silence as they all stood watching her.

Then the baby's arm moved.

The mother screamed.

"He's alive! He's alive!" she exclaimed. "I thought he was dead, but he's moving."

"Yes, he is alive," Celina replied, almost faint with relief. "Now you must keep breathing into his mouth yourself while we find him something to drink."

The woman gave another cry.

"It's a miracle. I thought he was dead."

"But we need milk," Celina said decisively. "Let someone run to the castle and tell the cook you have come from me and you want some milk. Then hurry back and we will save the child's life."

One of the men raced off. Now the women clustered round Celina, telling her their tales of hardship, how their babies had died or were sickly.

"And maybe it's best for the poor little mites to die," said one. "What kind of life can we give them?"

It felt like ages that Celina sat there talking, but mostly

listening. But there was no sign of her husband and her feeling of disquiet grew.

Where was he? Why did he not come?

At last, to her vast relief, she saw Robin riding quickly through the trees.

Silently she thanked God that he had come at last.

He was not alone. Behind him rode several other men and some of them were armed.

Egan Janner was there with two men from the stables who seemed to be guarding him suspiciously.

Of course! She should have foreseen this. Robin thought that she had been kidnapped and had come prepared to rescue her with violence if necessary.

That must not happen. She had made promises, telling these people that they could trust her and now she must not betray them.

A ripple of apprehension was beginning to run around the group. They too had understood the implications of this little posse.

Celina thought fast. Everything might depend on what happened now.

"Come with me," she said to the women on either side, "and bring your children. Let the men keep back."

As she spoke she took a baby from the arms of one of the women and began to advance towards where Robin was bringing his horse to a halt.

The two women followed her. To Celina's relief the men hung back as though understanding what was in her mind.

Robin had dismounted and was watching her approach with the child in her arms, frowning slightly. From the way he was standing she could see that his every nerve was on edge and he was ready to spring at any moment.

At all costs she must prevent a confrontation. If she seemed scared or upset there might be a disaster.

With a great effort she forced herself to look confident, even to smile,

"Thank goodness you have come! I was so afraid you might refuse and you are needed here more desperately than you have ever been wanted anywhere."

"What do you mean?" he growled. "Of course I came as soon as I received your note. How could you think I would ignore your danger?"

"But I am not in any danger. I am here of my own free will, so please tell your men to keep back and not to flaunt their weapons."

After staring for a moment Robin nodded and did as she asked.

"Do you give me your word that nobody has hurt you?" he insisted.

"Do I look hurt?" she asked with a well-judged air of surprise. "Of course nobody has harmed me. I am among friends here. As my friends, they have asked for my help and as their friend I have promised to give it to them."

She raised her voice deliberately so that everyone could hear what she had to say.

After a moment Robin nodded, indicating that he understood.

"But it would have been better if you had come for me yourself," he said. "You must understand that your note made me fear the worst."

Out of the corner of her eye she saw Egan Janner grow tense.

"I am sorry if I alarmed you, but I thought my time could be more usefully spent staying and learning about conditions here," she asserted firmly. "Mr. Janner kindly agreed to take my message."

She turned to the young man, still trapped between two armed grooms.

"Mr. Janner," she said, "thank you for fetching my husband. I am very grateful to you for the trouble you have taken."

At her friendly tone everybody seemed to relax and Janner gave a sigh of relief.

"So what is happening here?" Robin asked her. "I do not understand."

Quickly and urgently she explained and saw his face darken.

"This is intolerable and you may be sure that I shall put matters right. I had no idea – " Then he checked himself with a sound of impatience.

"But how did you come to be here in the first place?" he asked Celina.

"At my request," she said emphatically, "they brought me here to show me how much they are all suffering. Oh, Robin, please do something for them."

She spoke almost in a whisper, but her words were so intense that Robin put his arm round her shoulders.

"Of course I will. You were quite right to send for me. But why didn't you want me to bring my Steward?"

"Because this is all his doing," she cried fiercely. "While you have been in France he has done as he pleased, taken the money for himself and left these people with nothing."

"Is that what they say?"

"Yes, it is, and I believe them. I know you will have to talk to him, but I wanted you to see the reality before he starts making his excuses. Robin, there can be no excuse for letting people live in this state. I do not care how he tries to explain it. It is unforgivable."

"I agree, so you can calm down."

"No, I cannot calm down," she said passionately. "I will never be calm in the face of such a crime until I can see it put right."

She faced him.

"I have promised them that things will change," she said defiantly. "I have given them my word."

A strange look passed over his face, but all he said was,

"Have you, my dear?"

Then he moved to where several of them were standing in front of one of the broken-down cottages and said,

"I never expected to see such conditions on my land."

"There is plenty more to see," said Janner.

He started to walk away and as Robin followed him, the other men joined in, while Celina returned to the women.

She was still carrying the sick baby in her arms holding it closely against her breast, trying to warm it.

Suddenly, to her relief, she spied the man who had gone to fetch the milk. He was half running, half walking, so as not to spill the contents of a large jug.

"I've got it, I've got it," he yelled excitedly.

The women sent up a cry of joy.

She dropped a little of the milk into the baby's mouth and then a little more. With every drop the baby seemed to revive a little.

At last she handed the baby back to his mother, saying,

"Keep giving him just a little milk, only a little at a time, otherwise he might choke."

She looked around for Robin, hoping he would return to her soon. At last, after what seemed a long time, he appeared. At once the women crouching near Celina rose to their feet and ran towards him.

He stopped and faced them all. Celina noticed that his face was very pale, as though he had received a bad shock.

"I can only say how sorry I am that you have been treated in this appalling manner," he announced in a strained voice. "I had no idea and I promise you that your conditions will improve quickly.

"First and most important, you will all be paid what you are owed. Because of what you have been suffering, it will be doubled."

Everyone stared at Robin, but no one spoke and Celina realised that they were not convinced.

"I will send men to work on your cottages at my expense until they are all restored."

There was a feeble cheer that almost brought tears to Celina's eyes.

Several of the women started weeping and sighing,

"Thank you, thank you."

"And I promise you that this will never happen again," Robin assured them.

Egan Janner confronted him bravely.

"You say that, my Lord, but how can you be so sure? What happens next time you're away?"

"I will be here," Celina chimed in before Robin could reply.

She looked around at the assembled crowd in their dirty rags.

"You are under my protection now," she said loudly.

The response was a yell of delight.

Robin noted wryly that his wife's promise reassured them more than anything he could have said.

"Our children will live," cried one of the women through her tears. "And so will we."

"Of course you will," Celina said and added emphatically, "I know you will all feel grateful to his Lordship."

There was a brief, awkward silence. Then one or two of them raised an unconvincing cheer.

"Don't ask too much of them," Robin said wryly in her ear. "Why should they want to cheer me? I have only myself to blame."

"No, blame Stanley Halyard, your Steward." she retorted angrily.

Robin said nothing, but his thoughts were uncomfortable. It was he who had left the lazy Steward in charge, never asking questions as long as the estate prospered and he was free to indulge himself in France.

But this was something to be considered later, when he was alone and ready to confront himself honestly. For now there was work to be done.

He was about to tell Celina that it was time for them to leave when the sound of galloping hooves made them all look up.

A horse appeared in a cloud of dust, through which Stanley Halyard's furious face could be seen. As he reached them he jumped down to the ground, facing his employer in violent agitation.

"Is something the matter?" Robin asked coolly.

"I came at once to find out what's going on, my Lord," Halyard gasped. "What have these people been telling you?"

"What are you afraid they have been telling us?" Celina demanded boldly.

Halyard ignored her.

"My Lord, don't listen to their lies. You should have let me be here – "

"Should?" Robin's voice cut across him. "Are you giving me orders, Halyard?"

"No, my Lord – I didn't mean – "

Now Celina placed herself firmly in front of him.

"What Lord Torrington and I know we have learned from our own eyes. No words have been necessary."

Then Halyard made his biggest mistake.

"This has nothing to do with women," he bawled. "You don't know what you are talking about."

The next moment he was on the ground as Robin's fist connected with his chin. The crowd watching roared with delight and roared even louder as Robin leaned over, hauled the Steward to his feet and shook him like a rat.

"How dare you speak to Lady Torrington like that!" he shouted at him. "Now get on your horse and follow us back to the castle."

"My Lord, I protest," Halyard screamed. "These people are liars – the scum of the earth."

Robin released him so suddenly that he dropped to the ground. But he was up in a flash and ran to Janner.

"You were always a trouble maker," he howled. "I'll have you for this."

A nod from Robin made two of his outriders seize Halyard, dragging him away.

"Bring him back to the castle," he ordered. "But keep him away from me."

Then he turned to Celina.

"Allow me to assist you, madam," he said, holding out his arms.

She accepted his help onto White Fire's back and waited while he mounted his own horse.

As they turned to leave the people watching them gave a loud cheer.

Robin tried to remember when his people had ever showed such enthusiasm for him, but his mind was blank.

But of course, he realised, it was Celina they were cheering and not himself.

All the way home he had to ride faster to keep up with his wife.

"Are you trying to evade me, madam?" he asked quizzically.

"Of course not. It is just that I want to reach home as soon as possible so that I can arrange for food to be sent to those people at once. Things must be done quickly."

Without waiting for his answer she spurred her horse and was soon far ahead, leaving him to reflect that she was more of a surprise every day.

Who would have thought that deep inside Celina there was such a core of steel?

He could not help wondering whether the reason she had given for leaving him behind was the true one? Did she despise him for what he had allowed to happen while he was away, thinking only of his own pleasures?

And if she did, what answer could he possibly give her?

As the castle came in sight Celina urged her horse on faster. A groom appeared by the front door to wait for her and she jumped down, tossing him her reins.

"Do we have a large cart in the stables?" she asked.

"Yes, my Lady."

"Good. I want it brought round to the kitchen entrance at once," she ordered briskly.

Then she hurried inside and straight to the kitchens.

Mrs. Crale, the cook and the butler's wife, looked up in surprise.

"A cart is coming round in a minute," Celina said. "It

is to collect food for the tenants and I would like you to fill it to the brim. Just keep enough for our needs until tomorrow and order more food to be delivered immediately."

"You leave it to me, my Lady," the cook nodded.

"Also a couple of footmen to accompany the cart."

"I'll have a word with my husband," Mrs. Crale promised.

Luckily Crale was entering the kitchen at that moment. Celina explained the position, being as brief and businesslike as she could.

"The footmen will need to oversee the distribution of the food," she said. "And perhaps they should be as plainly dressed as possible. Formal clothes and powdered wigs would be out of place there."

"As your Ladyship commands," Crale said respectfully. "I will choose the biggest and strongest lads we have and, with your permission, I'll send four men, not two. I know that place and it's bad."

"It's only bad because of the way they have been treated," Celina said. "But you are right, four would be better. Please send for me when everything is ready."

"What will Mr. Halyard say?" one of the kitchen maids mused in awe.

"You mind your tongue, my girl," the cook said sharply. "It's nothing to you what he says."

"In any case, you can leave me to deal with Mr. Halyard," Celina added and departed, unaware of leaving her audience bereft of words.

In the hall she found an elderly footman and asked him,

"Has his Lordship returned yet?"

"Yes, my Lady. He and Mr. Halyard went to the library."

"Excellent," Celina said crisply, and swept on to the library at such a pace that the footman had to hurry ahead to open the door for her.

To her disappointment Celina found Robin completely alone.

"I thought Mr. Halyard was with you," she exclaimed.

"He was, but I sent him about his business. At this very moment he is on his way to his cottage, accompanied by my secretary and two armed men. They will secure all his books and receipts and see him off the premises."

Accurately reading her expression, he remarked with a gleam of humour,

"I appreciate that you wished to engage him in mortal combat yourself, but it seemed better to be rid of him as soon as possible."

"Oh, well, never mind," she said with a shrug. "I admit I would have enjoyed throwing him out, but I don't suppose it matters which of us does it."

Her husband did not answer this, but his face was reflective.

"I hope you engage a new Steward soon," she said. "There is so much to organise, not just the repair of the cottages, but urgent medical attention for the people. In fact, a doctor should visit them this afternoon."

"You want to send Dr. Everard to that place?" he asked, startled.

Celina considered for a moment.

"No, I have little faith in Dr. Everard. To my mind he is nothing but a pompous, social climbing creature, more concerned with acquiring important patients than with being a good doctor."

"That is just a little harsh since you hardly know him," Robin observed mildly.

"I know that his diagnoses tend to be in line with what his wealthy clients wish to believe," she replied at once. "Robin, have you never wondered why he didn't see through your mother's 'illness'?"

"What?"

"If he had been doing his job properly, she could not have fooled him for a moment."

She gave a wicked chuckle.

"And if he had spotted the truth, you would have been spared the dreadful fate of having to marry me. That alone should make you annoyed with him."

For once Robin was totally speechless. He had almost forgotten his grudge about the way he had been fooled, but now he realised that everything Celina said was right.

All he could think of was how unimportant it all seemed now. His mind was full of the shocking sights he had witnessed today. Which was, he realised, exactly what his alarming, unpredictable and thrilling wife had wanted.

"So you do not think that Dr. Everard is good enough?" he managed to say at last.

"Not for my friends."

"Just good enough for the Torrington family?" he asked sardonically.

"That, of course, is for you to say," Celina replied demurely. "You are the Master here."

"Am I?" he could not resist asking.

"Of course. How could anyone doubt it?"

"Are you making fun of me, madam?"

"Do you think I am?"

"I no longer know what I think about anything, except that I do not think I would dare argue with you."

Celina gave him a charming smile.

"Excellent. That will save time. I really cannot entrust this mission to Dr. Everard. I will call in Dr. Landon, who has been my doctor and Uncle James's for many years. I had better write him a note now, asking him to call on the tenants quickly and promising that I will pay his fees."

She looked around for paper, but Robin was ahead of her, ushering her into the chair at his own desk, pushing a sheet of Torrington headed writing paper towards her, dipping his pen in the ink and handing it to her, like a dutiful secretary.

"Everard will have a fit when he finds out," he observed.

"That cannot be helped," she said, beginning to write. "I prefer Dr. Landon because I know him and have considerable faith in him."

She was unaware of the effect she was producing on Robin, but the cool way she said "I prefer" made him gaze at her, eyebrows raised.

He was seeing a new woman, a clear-headed, decisive woman who did not look to him for authority, but coolly overrode him when it suited her.

She finished the letter, signed it with a confident flourish and put it in an envelope. With a smile Robin handed her the Torrington seal.

"You may find this effective," he suggested.

"Thank you," she agreed, affixing the seal and ringing the little bell on his desk.

A footman appeared and she gave him the letter with directions where it was to be taken.

"And I have been asked to inform you, my Lady, that the cart is ready, as you required."

"Thank you. Tell them I am coming at once."

"You are going out again?" Robin asked in

consternation as the footman left the room.

"I must. I need to be there when the food arrives and I want to talk to the doctor as well."

"I think you should stay here and talk to me. We have much to discuss."

"Have we? I would have thought it had all been said."

"Upon my word, madam, you *are* a cool one."

"Well, a cool head is what is needed in a time of crisis. Is that not so?"

"And just how long do you intend to stay away?"

"As long as it takes."

"May I remind you that we are guests of honour at a dinner tonight?"

"Heavens, so we are! Thank you, I had forgotten."

Robin ground his teeth.

"I am happy to have been of service. Please hurry home. You will need at least two hours to be ready."

"Two hours? Surely not. What can possibly take two hours? I have never taken two hours to dress in my life."

"You were not the Countess of Torrington before. At the height of her social life my mother always took at least two hours."

"Why?" she asked, genuinely puzzled.

"Because she was Lady Torrington," he said, his voice rising.

"I am Lady Torrington and one hour is enough," she retorted, also speaking more loudly. "I shall be home in good time."

"Celina, will you please – ?"

But he was talking to empty air.

CHAPTER NINE

Celina scurried out of the library and down the steps to where the rest of the party was ready for her.

She paused for a moment to check that all was as she had commanded, and was pleased to see that the cart was full with four plainly dressed footmen in attendance.

"Excellent," she said crisply, leaping into her saddle. "Let us be on our way."

She would never forget the cheer that greeted them as they came in sight of the village. It confirmed what she already knew – that the people there had not expected her to return. Now that she had done so they were overwhelmed with joy and relief.

To increase her pleasure Dr. Landon arrived, driving his little carriage that was filled with medical supplies. Celina advanced to him with her hand outstretched.

They had a serious talk which culminated in her guiding him into a disused cottage.

"It will have to be restored, but then it would be suitable for a weekly clinic. I believe you have recently taken on an assistant. Once you have seen all these people and made the initial diagnoses you might feel able to delegate routine visits to him. But, of course, I leave those decisions to you."

"You do?" he asked, unable to contain his surprise.

He did not realise it, but he was reacting exactly as Robin had done, a couple of hours earlier.

She gave him her most charming smile.

"I am sorry if I seem to be simply marching over you," she said, "But it's so – "

"Please don't apologise," he replied quickly. "If you only knew how good it is to see someone prepared to do something for these poor creatures – "

Out of the corner of her eye Celina became aware that a man on horseback was watching them. It was Robin, sitting there very quiet and still. She wondered how long he had been there and how much he had heard.

He greeted the doctor pleasantly, declared himself glad that the estate was to employ his services and pronounced all the arrangements excellent.

"Now, my dear, it is time for us to be going home," he said.

"You came to fetch me?"

"I was afraid you would become so absorbed in your work that you would forget me altogether," he replied smoothly. "Let us hurry now or Mama will be anxious."

On reaching the castle Celina ran straight up to her room where she found a positive entourage of maids and dressers waiting for her.

"You have been longer than I expected, my Lady," Nora sniffed. "And your clothes are in a dirty state. Where have you been to get in such a mess?"

Celina envisaged the children who had been sitting on her lap and who had to endure dirt and rags every day.

But then she forced herself to concentrate on the evening ahead. She had a job to do. It was called being Lady Torrington and there was more than one way to do it.

She had a bath, scrubbing away the stains of the tragic

village from her body, although not banishing them from her mind. Then she concentrated on clothes.

Her gown was ivory, made of satin with lace flounces, tailored in the latest fashion. When she was dressed everyone stood back and regarded her with awe.

"Oh, my Lady!" Nora sighed. "You look so – so – "

"Yes, indeed she does," agreed a voice from the door.

They all whirled to see Robin standing in the doorway, resplendent in evening dress. He advanced into the room, his eyes fixed on Celina.

"It needs but one more item to complete the picture," he said, opening the jewel box he was carrying.

Celina gasped at the sight of the magnificent Torrington pearls – a tiara, a necklace and ear-rings.

"I have so looked forward to seeing these heirlooms adorn my daughter-in-law," said the Dowager, just behind her son. "And now my dearest wish is fulfilled."

Celina turned to view herself in the long mirror and was overcome by the sight. Now she truly looked like the Countess of Torrington.

And she *was* beautiful. There was no doubt about it.

She wondered if Robin thought so. He was smiling but in a way that gave nothing away.

He gave her his arm and they walked downstairs, followed by the Dowager. There, waiting for them, was the grand Torrington carriage, with the family crest on both panels.

Beresford Manor was only a couple of miles away and soon they were turning into the main gate, from where they could see the big house flooded with light.

It was an evening out of her dreams. She was the bride of Torrington, the guest of honour whom everyone wanted to see. And if only she could have been bathing in her husband's love, everything would have been perfection.

Everyone for miles around had come to see the new Countess. Although Lord Beresford was a mere Viscount, his wife was more highly connected and all the local nobility had assembled to welcome the new couple.

"And my dear brother absolutely insisted on joining us," Lady Beresford simpered.

For a moment Celina's mind became blank as she struggled to recall who her brother was. It was Robin's muttered, "oh, good grief!" that reminded her.

"It will be a pleasure to see Lord Delaine," she said with a forced smile. "I have such happy memories of our acquaintance."

"Well it's more than I do," Robin growled as they turned away. "He had better behave himself."

"Don't be so stuffy," she whispered back. "He is more likely to make a clown of himself than be offensive."

"Some men can manage both," he riposted.

This proved to be an understatement. Lord Delaine wore black, as if in mourning, grabbed the seat next to Celina and made sheep's eyes at her throughout the meal.

When the dancing began he would have led her onto the floor, had not Robin intimidated him with a furious glance. After that he consoled himself with brandy.

"May I hope for the first dance?" Robin murmured.

"Of course," she said demurely. "Everyone is expecting it."

A small burst of applause confirmed this, as he took her into his arms for the first waltz.

"And you are *not* going to dance with *him* tonight," he growled.

"Don't worry. He will be under the table in a few minutes!"

"So maybe you made the right choice in refusing him?"

"I am not sure. A husband who could be relied on to vanish under the table might be very convenient at times."

She looked up into his face, teasing him with her smile.

"Perhaps I did make an unwise choice," she mused.

He tightened his grip, drawing her close to him.

"You will drive me too far, madam."

"But how far is too far?" she quizzed him.

"Knowing you, I am sure you are determined to find out."

"But you don't know me," she whispered. "You never did."

The truth of her statement left him bereft of speech for a moment.

If there was one thing that today had proved, it was that he did *not* know her.

"I am grateful to you," he said unexpectedly. "You showed me much that I should have discovered for myself. I should never have stayed away so long."

"Don't upset yourself," Celina said. "After all, you had every right to stay in France, if that is where you wanted to be."

Robin nodded abstractedly. It was, of course, true that he had the right to please himself, and if his wife had said otherwise he would have declared firmly that she was wrong.

But, hearing her take his side, he felt a most irrational instinct to argue. He had failed, claiming the pleasures of his position but leaving the duties to others, and she ought to berate him for it like any other wife.

But she was not like any other wife. He was beginning to understand that fact.

"From now on, I will stay here to keep my eyes on the estate," he said.

"But there is no need now that I have it all in hand," she pointed out. "I have promised the tenants that I will be here for them and I will be keeping my word."

"Does that mean you have decided to stay?" he asked. "It was only recently that you were threatening to end our marriage."

She considered.

"But I cannot leave now," she stated firmly. "I have given them my word and I must not let them down. Of course I shall stay."

"Thank you for informing me," he responded stiffly. "It is certainly a relief to know that my wife intends to remain under my roof, even if I am the last to know."

"I am glad you are pleased. So now that everything is sorted out, you can return to France with an easy conscience."

She was playing a subtle but dangerous game. The last thing she wanted was for Robin to return to France, but she knew that any hint of a desire to restrain him would be fatal.

But if he thought she was happy for him to go, that might – it just might – intrigue him enough to make him stay.

To her delight he sounded chagrined as he said,

"Are you giving me your permission, madam?"

Robin spoke the words in his most frozen voice. It was a voice that had intimidated many people, but Celina seemed untroubled by it.

"Well, I am sure you have important business to attend to in Paris," she said brightly.

Was there a hint of irony in her voice? he wondered.

Important business? Surely everyone knew why he went to Paris? But this was not the kind of subject a man could really discuss his wife.

He saw her watching him, her face bland and innocent.

Suspiciously innocent, he told himself.

His first thought was that she need not think she could influence him. His second was that she was really incredible. What other woman had ever challenged him in such a fashion?

His third thought was that she might actually be eager to see him go, so that she could have a free hand on the estate.

If that was what she imagined, she would be disappointed. He had just resolved to remain.

He was beginning to wonder if being married might be more interesting than he had expected.

After that conversation Celina danced with almost every man present, but not Lord Delaine, who had been carried away soon after the meal.

Robin performed his duty, leading onto the floor his hostess and various other ladies who would be insulted if he had ignored them. But wherever he was, whoever he was dancing with, he was always acutely aware of his wife in the arms of some other man.

Often he would try to glance at her quickly, without being too obvious about it, and he could not delude himself that she was suffering without him.

On the contrary, she seemed to be having a very good time, not only dancing but chattering with her partners. Sometimes she would burst out laughing.

Once he saw her sitting down, engaged in deep conversation with an elderly uncle of the family, one who was known to take a great interest in estate management.

For some reason this was even worse. Robin had an uneasy feeling that Celina was discussing strategy.

"What a delightful evening," his mother said to him once. "Isn't it wonderful to see our dear Celina such a success?"

"Wonderful," her son agreed darkly.

The evening stretched on and on, for everyone wanted to talk to the marvellous new Countess. But at last all the goodbyes were said and they were free to enter their carriage and start the journey home.

As Robin had feared, Celina had been learning from the elderly uncle and was full of ideas. She leaned back against the squabs, smiling happily, making plans.

"Well done, my dear!" the Dowager said. "Your first big occasion and you did so well. I do hope you enjoyed the evening."

"Tremendously!" Celina murmured. "I really enjoyed talking to Sir Watkins."

"I do hope he didn't bore you too much."

"Not at all," Celina replied. "He was most helpful."

"I have dismissed Halyard, Mama," Robin said. "He has been mistreating my tenants."

"I heard that there was some commotion going on today," she admitted. "But not the details."

He began to explain it all to her.

Listening to their soft voices talking, Celina let herself sink into the mists of sleep that were enveloping her. It had been a long tiring day and now she felt that she was floating in another realm.

At last Robin and his mother fell silent, which was a relief to him because he wanted to reflect on what had happened today. And especially he wanted to reflect on the extraordinary woman who had become his wife, but whom, he now understood, was a total stranger to him.

That discovery came as a shock. He had thought he

knew her well. She was pretty enough and charming, but not exceptional. Certainly she could not compare with the brilliant beauties with whom he had always entertained himself.

So he had thought – in his arrogance.

But today Celina had made him see her in a different light, first as a woman of character and authority, then as a beauty, able to hold her own in company and win the admiration of the County.

He had always said that one of the great delights of life was to meet a totally new woman.

But when that totally new woman turned out to be his wife, the pleasure of anticipation was almost unbearably poignant.

Of course, they were only at the beginning. They had a long road to travel yet. But now he was intrigued by that road, where he had only been exasperated earlier.

When he thought of how enchanting she had looked tonight, he felt a stirring deep within himself. She was his wife and he could no longer wait to make love to her. He wondered if she too felt any different towards him.

If he met her eyes now, what would he find in them? Tonight – would there be an invitation? He felt his heart begin to beat faster as he turned his head towards her.

She was fast asleep.

Dumbfounded, Robin stared into her face, but there was no escaping the fact that Celina's response to an evening of triumphant success was to become dead to the world.

Or was she trying to tell him something?

A few minutes later the carriage pulled up. The door opened and arms reached inside to assist the Dowager to descend.

Robin, who had continued to watch Celina intently,

touched her arm. She smiled and gave a little sigh, but did not open her eyes.

Driven by something he only half understood, he leaned forward and laid his lips on hers. At once he felt her sway towards him, so that her head rested on his shoulder.

The next moment he had enfolded her in a passionate embrace.

She was pure sweetness in his arms, her lips moving softly on his, her body relaxed and yielding against him. Other women had teased and tormented him, deliberately inflaming his desire for their own ends.

She was different. There was nothing calculated about her, he realised. Everything was spontaneous, generous and heartfelt, and she was causing a flowering in his heart that he had never thought possible.

How could there be such joy?

With her. Only with her.

But, to his horror, he became aware of sounds behind him and he returned to the real world to realise that he was passionately embracing his wife, to the amusement of his servants.

"Her Ladyship was asleep," he stammered. "I was waking her."

Celina opened her eyes, smiling sleepily.

"We are home," he said. "Let me help you out."

She put her hand in his, allowed him to help her down and clinging to his arm walked with him into the castle.

"Goodnight, my dears," the Dowager called.

She was already climbing the stairs.

They followed slowly, heading for Celina's room. There was still a soft smile on her face and her husband wondered just how much she remembered. Had she even been aware that he had kissed her?

Never mind. He would make her aware of it.

Nora was waiting inside the great bedroom, but Robin dismissed her with a nod, drawing his wife's cloak from her shoulders with his own hands.

Celina sighed.

"If only – I could remember – "

"Remember what?" he asked eagerly.

"This evening – something – on the way home – "

"Yes – yes – ?"

"It came to me – and then it slipped away – if only I could remember – "

"Try," he urged.

He ventured to lay his hands on her shoulders, striving for her to meet his eyes so that they could exchange glances when she remembered. He began drawing her towards him –

"Ah!" she said. "That's it?"

"You know what it is?"

"Yes, it was when you were telling your mother about Mr. Halyard when the answer suddenly came to me. You will need a new Steward and I know the perfect one."

He grew still.

"What?" he asked in a hollow voice.

"Mr. Bramley. He is now Uncle James's Steward, but he is always complaining that he does not have enough to do, with the estate being so small. He is efficient and honest and I am sure Uncle James will understand us taking him away."

"I am quite sure that he will," the Earl said, dropping his hands. "You will explain the matter to him and he will hurry to obey you, the way everyone has done."

"Of course, you will have to meet him – "

"A mere formality, I assure you."

"But truly, it's a wonderful idea. He is just what we want."

For a wild moment Robin contemplated telling her exactly what he wanted – and how far away Mr. Bramley was from being about to provide it.

But the impulse died and a feeling of defeat came over him.

"Of course," he said in a dead voice, "it is an excellent notion and I know that I can leave everything to you. Why don't you write to him immediately?"

"What a good idea! Oh, you are so clever! I will do it now."

Robin drew himself up, stiff with affronted dignity.

"In that case, madam, I shall bid you goodnight and trouble you no further."

His head high, he left the room through the connecting door, taking care to lock it behind him.

*

By dawn's early light Celina awoke and lay thinking about the night before.

There was one vision that troubled her – herself in the carriage, feeling her husband draw her into his arms to kiss her – the sensation of his lips on hers –

And then the vision had vanished and she was back in the coach, letting him hand her down.

Had it happened? Or had it all been a dream?

She had meant to find the answer when they were alone together in her room. Surely she could tempt him to kiss her again?

If he had really kissed her the first time.

But if he had not –

Could she take the risk?

At the last moment her nerve had failed her and she had resorted to a stratagem. All the time she had spoken about the new Steward, she had been hoping Robin would lose patience and seize her in his arms.

Instead he had accepted her decision in a most uninspiring way.

Now she was desolate. He did not want her after all.

But there were those who did, she reminded herself. She had promised to stay for their sake and there was work to be done.

As soon as she entered the breakfast room, she saw Robin sitting at the table. He gave her a polite smile.

"Did you send the note to Mr. Bramley?" he enquired.

"I have just given it to a footman."

"Good. Then things will move. When you have settled the matter with him, bring him to me. In the meantime I shall be making financial arrangements for that little medical practice you have set up."

"I do have some money of my own. I was thinking that I could – "

"That would be quite inappropriate. This is for me to pay for. I beg you not to insult me by suggesting otherwise."

That silenced her.

After their conversation, events moved smoothly.

Mr. Bramley came with all speed and professed himself delighted with his new post. Uncle James had taken the opportunity to come too and was all compliance.

"I was bound to lose him sooner or later," he confided to Celina. "My estate is not big enough to occupy his considerable talents. But this will keep him in the neighbourhood and he can still come and play chess with me sometimes."

He accompanied Mr. Bramley to Robin's office and

the three men drank a toast to the new order. Celina left them to it, recognising that it was wiser to involve Robin in her new arrangements. For the sake of the tenants she needed him on her side.

Feeling suddenly alone she wandered into the library, where there would be some newspapers to read.

She flicked through the day's delivery and then, to her surprise, discovered that some were in French. The most recent newspaper was dated only a week ago, which suggested that Robin was having them sent over from France.

Why? Could it be that his heart was still in France. Was there a woman there who still wrote to him?

She tried to believe that she was making too much of a few newspapers, but she could not stop herself opening them feverishly and scanning the print for anything that might be relevant to her husband.

And there was his name.

She stared, certain that she must have been mistaken.

But there was no mistake. The story concerned Lord Torrington, an English '*milord*' who was a frequent visitor to the city of Paris, where he was known as a lavish spender of money and a lover of many beautiful women.

Celina gave a soft little sigh.

The story mentioned a man called Pierre Vallon, who had been sent to prison two years ago for stealing fabulous jewellery from the dancer Marie Lemans.

Lord Torrington, known to be one of her admirers, had played a part in Vallon's capture and testified against him in court, as a result of which he had been given a long prison sentence.

As he was dragged away from the court he had screamed,

"I'll come back. I'll get my revenge and it will break your heart."

"Nonsense, he has no heart," somebody had quipped.

Everyone had laughed at this and the '*milord*' had laughed more heartily than anyone.

Now, it seemed, Vallon had escaped from jail and vanished.

There was a small drawing of him, showing him to have a shaven head and a heavy moustache. The artist was sufficiently skilled to catch a vicious gleam in his eye. This would be a terrible man to have as an enemy, Celina realised.

She drew in a sharp breath, her heart beating with fear.

The next moment she heard a sound outside the door and hurried tucked the newspaper away, beneath the others.

Robin looked in, smiling.

"We have guests for lunch," he said. "I know you will be glad that your uncle and Mr. Bramley are staying."

"Yes – yes, of course."

"Good Heavens, what is the matter with you?" he asked, looking at her in concern.

"Nothing – nothing."

"This is your moment of triumph. You have everyone doing your bidding, including me."

"Nonsense! As though I cared – "

She longed to tell him that nothing mattered except his safety, but she could not utter the words.

How could she tell him that she loved him and her heart was breaking at the thought of the secret life he concealed from her?

His life was in danger, but he would not tell her. She might lose him at any moment.

"Let's go to lunch," he said.

The rest of the day was devoted to business and, from that point of view, was extremely satisfactory.

After lunch they all travelled to the village and Celina was able to explain exactly what she wanted the new Steward to do.

He nodded and seemed impressed by her clear mind.

It was, as Robin had said, her moment of triumph, but it was hard to remember that when she was full of fear.

Pierre Vallon had threatened her husband's life. He was out there somewhere, waiting for the moment to kill him.

She watched Robin, trembling as she felt a cloud of death hanging over him, wondering what the future held.

*

Uncle James stayed to supper, but left early, saying that he was an old man and needed an early night.

Later Celina walked slowly to her room, worn out with the effort of trying to appear bright and normal.

'I love him,' she told herself. 'But how can I make him love me? Whatever is going to happen to us?'

The room was in darkness, save for a flickering light on the dressing table.

Slowly she walked to one of the windows and pulled back the curtains. Immediately the light from the moon flowed into the room, bathing everything in a soft silver that reflected her melancholy mood.

Suddenly a shadow reared up behind the window and the air was rent with the sound of smashing glass. She jumped back with a shriek as a man's arm came through the broken window, groping towards her.

Then the rest of him appeared, his leg, his body and his head.

At the sight of his face she screamed. She had seen the

shaven head and dark glinting eyes in the French newspaper.

This was Pierre Vallon – the man who was set on murdering her husband.

"Go away," she cried hoarsely. "*Go away*."

His face terrified her. It was dark and bitter, filled with hate and vengeance.

"I know who you are," he said, speaking in English but with a heavy accent.

"That – doesn't matter – "

"You're his wife. I read about your wedding in the paper. Very sudden. He must be madly in love with you, and that's just what I want."

She could almost have laughed, bitterly. Madly in love with her. If only he were!

"Get out of here," she yelled, backing away from him. "Get out!"

On the words she turned and tried to escape. If only she could reach the door!

There was only one thought in her mind. She must not let him reach Robin. Only her husband mattered. Whatever it cost her, she would protect him.

But Vallon threw himself onto her, carrying her to the ground. She screamed and screamed again, until his hand over her mouth silenced her.

He rolled off her onto the floor and yanked her up so that he was holding her with his hands around her throat.

"I told him I'd make him suffer," he croaked hoarsely. "I said I'd break his heart, and I have waited until now – to escape – to get my revenge – waiting – waiting – "

She tried to speak but his hands tightened around her neck.

"Now I can do it because his heart is yours – "

"No – no – you're wrong – he doesn't love me – "

"Liar!"

"No – I love him, but he cares nothing for me – "

"You don't fool me. He's madly in love with you, I know it. He was wild about Marie Lemans and she betrayed him with me. He had me locked away in prison. That was his revenge. But now I am here for *my* revenge and I will take it with the woman who means more to him than Marie ever did."

As if from a great distance she heard a door open. Her head was swimming, she was losing consciousness, but she must not give in. Robin was in danger – she must save him – she must –

"Get away from her."

It was Robin's voice. She could not see him, but she could see the face of Pierre Vallon as he looked up and beheld the man he hated. A look of evil joy came into his eyes.

His hand moved fast and the next second he was holding a knife.

"You'll be here to see her die," he gloated. "That makes it perfect."

"I said let her go."

But Vallon only laughed. It was a dreadful sound, and it seemed to fill the whole world.

Slowly he raised the hand with the knife.

The darkness was closing on Celina. From somewhere she heard a shout and the next moment a body came flying through the air to land on Vallon, dragging him away from her, fighting him madly.

"No – " she whispered. "He will kill you – stay away, my love – "

Then she lost consciousness.

CHAPTER TEN

It was a long time later that Celina opened her eyes.

At first she did not know where she was, except that she was in a room she had never seen before. She tried to turn her head, but her neck was painful.

Then to her astonishment she heard Robin say gently,

"Are you all right, darling? Speak to me if you can."

Darling? Had he really said that word?

He was looking down at her, his eyes full of anxiety.

"Tell me that you can hear me," he begged.

Now Celina remembered what had happened. Pierre Vallon had leapt through the window and seized her. He had drawn a knife, but her husband had thrown open the door and hurled himself into terrible danger to save her.

After that she had known no more.

She wanted to ask him a million questions, but her throat was very painful and it was impossible, for the moment, to speak.

But he was alive. As he leaned over to kiss her very softly and she felt his lips on hers, she was overwhelmed by relief.

"Tell me you are not hurt," she pleaded in a hoarse whisper. "He held a knife."

"Which he was going to use on you. I had to stop him."

"And you did. You saved my life. You could have been killed – "

"What would I care if you were in such peril?" he said fervently. "Forget that man. He is dead."

"*Dead*? But how – ?"

"While we were fighting for the knife, he managed to wrench himself free and run for the window. I don't know if he had forgotten the long drop or whether he no longer cared what happened to him, but he landed hard on the flagstones below and died instantly."

"Then you are safe," she cried joyfully.

"And so are you, which is what really matters."

"Safe," she whispered longingly. "If only – oh, there's so much I do not understand – "

"Don't worry about it now. Just think about getting well, and then – " he checked himself, "well – then – "

"Yes?" she asked eagerly.

"All in good time. There are questions we must talk about, but only when you have regained your strength."

Reluctantly she accepted that she would have to be patient, although it would be very hard. With a sigh she lay back on the pillow.

"Where am I?" she asked. "I don't know this room."

"This is my room. I had you brought in here because I thought the sight of yours might upset you with so many bad memories."

"Thank you so much. It was kind of you to think of that."

She wanted to ask him so much. More than that, she wanted to enjoy the wonder of him being here with her. But suddenly he rose and moved away to talk to someone else who was in the room.

As the other man drew closer, she saw that it was Dr. Landon.

"It is good to see you awake again," he said. "Your neck is badly bruised, but it will heal. For the moment you must have complete rest and try not to talk too much."

As they walked to the door Celina wanted to cry out to Robin to stay with her, but she could make no sound.

There was so much to say and yet so much that she did not know how to say.

She remembered telling Vallon that her husband did not love her, although she loved him. Robin had appeared almost at once, but how much had he heard?

Did he know her secret now?

If so and he did not love her, how could she ever face him?

But there had been something in his voice as he ordered Vallon to get away from her that had stirred her heart.

Might he love her *after all*?

If there was even the faintest chance of his love, she felt as if she would die from too much happiness.

She tried to read his expression as he returned to her, just managing to reach out and touch his hand.

"You have been wonderful," he said. "That devil meant to kill us both."

"I read about him in the newspaper," she murmured. "I knew who he was. I was so afraid that he would kill you. He said terrible things about seeking his revenge, and about you – "

"Never mind that now," he said quickly. "Just try to sleep."

144

He raised her hand up to his lips and kissed it. Then he said,

"I promise you, you are quite safe now and no one will dare come near you."

He walked to the door and for a moment he looked back at her and next he was gone.

'He saved me,' she thought, 'just as I saved him. He kissed my hand and he said that I was wonderful. But did he say that he loved me? If only I could remember.'

Her mind was clouded and she could not recall whether he had spoken those crucial words. He had said that he was grateful to her, but gratitude was not love.

'I want his love,' she murmured to herself. 'But what will happen now? Since his enemy is dead, perhaps he will return to Paris. How can I bear to lose him when I love him *so* much?'

Still murmuring, 'I love him,' she fell asleep.

She was not aware that Robin had entered the room and came to stand by the bed, looking down at her.

When he saw that she was fast asleep, he leaned down and kissed her on the mouth, so softly that she did not awaken. Then he left the room quietly so as not to disturb her.

*

It was nearly five days before the doctor allowed Celina to get up and sit by the open window.

After another two days she was allowed out on to the balcony.

Nora attended her constantly. So did the Dowager, but neither of them would allow Celina to look into her own bedroom.

"It is being completely redecorated," the Dowager told her, "so that there will never be anything to remind you of what happened. And Robin's orders are that you are not to enter the room until it is finished."

She laughed and clapped her hands.

"He is taking so much trouble. It's quite delightful to see him. But don't tell him I told you that."

Before she left the room she turned back and gave Celina a long intent look. She had done the same many times in the last few days, Celina realised, as though she were studying her for some reason.

"Is something wrong, ma'am?" Celina asked.

"No, my dear, nothing at all. I am just leaving."

She whisked herself out of the room before Celina could ask her any more questions.

Whenever she saw Robin she insisted that she was better and wanted to get up.

"It is too soon," he always said. "I want to take no chances."

They did not speak of love, but his manner to her was always gentle and tender. Several times a day he would come and sit with her and talk about nothing very much, almost as if merely being with her was a pleasure to him.

One evening he told her that he had been to see the tenants and the cottages were being rebuilt in the village while the children were growing stronger every day.

"I am so pleased," Celina enthused. "I have been thinking about them and wondering how they were faring."

"All is well now. When you see the progress you will be so pleased."

"I knew that you would make everything right on the estate," Celina replied.

"It was not me who did that, but you. When I go there they crowd around asking how you are. I have had to promise to take you to see them soon."

"How kind they are!"

"No one has earned their gratitude more than you. I almost forgot to tell you that a new baby has arrived and they have named it after you."

Celina gave a soft laugh.

"It should really be your name," she said.

"Actually it is a girl," Robin replied with a smile. "But I will have my turn when one of the women produces a boy. In the meantime I have sent 'baby Celina' a present from both of us. It is just a little necklace that I bought in the village, not very expensive, but it gave the mother a great deal of pleasure."

"I want to get up *now*," Celina said.

"The doctor says you can tomorrow but you are not to leave the house or do anything too strenuous."

"Tomorrow," Celina exclaimed. "Then I will be able to have luncheon with you and perhaps dinner."

Robin smiled.

"It all depends on how you feel," he said, "and actually I have something to show you as soon as you are strong enough."

"Does that mean that my room is finished?" she asked.

He pretended surprise.

"What do you know about that?"

"Nothing at all," she said with a smile. "But I am still longing to see it."

"Mama has had a wonderful time choosing wallpaper."

"It was so kind of you to think of me," she replied, "but I have been very happy sleeping in your bed except that I worried that you were uncomfortable."

"I was only uncomfortable," Robin answered, "because I was worrying about you. As for thinking about

147

you – yes, I have been doing that a lot, although not, perhaps, as much as I should have done."

She tried to see his eyes, but suddenly he could not look at her. He seemed awkward and uneasy.

"I must go now," he said. "I will see you again later."

When he had gone Celina lay wondering about a new note she had heard in his voice. Something was about to happen between them, she was sure of it. Something new and thrilling!

She prayed that by some miracle he would be learning to love her. If it did not happen now –

But she could not bear to think about that.

Nora came to help Celina dress, bringing one of her more elegant new gowns.

'Please,' she prayed, 'let him think me beautiful. Let this wonderful time last. I love him so much.'

When he came to fetch her she crossed her fingers, hoping to find admiration in his eyes. But all she saw was that he was looking serious and wondered if she had been deluding herself.

"How are you feeling?" he asked quietly.

"I feel very well," she assured him.

"Good. Now I have something to show you. Will you come with me?"

"Of course I will."

She tried to speak confidently, but she felt a sudden fear that perhaps he was preparing her for his departure abroad again.

Instead of going to her bedroom, he led her out into the corridor and up the stairs, walking very slowly in case it was too much for her.

Finally, when she thought they were nearly at the top of the castle, he stopped in front of an oak door.

She was full of misgiving. Now she recalled a rumour she had once heard that Robin kept a special suite of rooms in the castle, which he had built for one of his favourite Parisian mistresses.

No other woman had ever been invited to stay, but this one was different. He had, reputedly, been wild about her, even inviting to stay at the castle while his mother was away.

All the servants and some of his friends had known that she was there. They had even expected him to marry her.

But there had been no marriage. She had left and returned to France and never been heard of again.

She remembered Vallon's words about Marie Lemans, how wildly Robin had loved her and how bitterly he had taken his revenge when she betrayed him.

Now Celina wondered if her husband wanted her to realise how much Marie Lemans had meant to him, and that she was still his true love, more important than his wife.

Perhaps she was dead and this room was a shrine to her memory.

As she stood there, waiting in trepidation, he said,

"In this room there is something very dear to my heart. Now I want you to see it."

Celina drew in her breath. Every nerve in her body made her want to run away and say she had no wish to hear any more.

She wanted to cry out 'no, spare me this. Let me live in the belief of your affection, even if it is only an illusion.'

But she could not say the words.

Besides, that was the coward's way and so she would force herself to be strong enough to endure whatever there was to be faced.

"Very well," she muttered quietly. "I will see whatever you wish me to see."

"Did you ever hear a rumour that I was once madly in love?"

"You have been the subject of so many rumours," she said, trying to delay the evil moment.

"But you have heard this one?"

"Yes, I have heard this one."

"I have brought you here so that you can see the woman who captured my heart and made it hers for eternity."

Something in the way he spoke was so moving that Celina felt her heart reach out to him. She wanted to run away and back down the stairs they had just climbed.

But she would not allow herself such weakness.

Robin handed her the key of the door in front of them. For a moment she was tempted to throw it down on the floor.

But she forced herself to put the key in the lock and turn it.

The door swung open at once. At first it was impossible for Celina to see what was inside.

Then she realised that they were in the central tower of the castle in a large room. It was empty, save for a picture on an easel.

The sun was coming through the windows of the tower, shining onto the picture at which she dared not look.

This was the woman her husband loved and he had brought her here to make her realise that he would never love anyone else.

Including herself. Or perhaps, most of all, herself.

"I want you to look at this picture," Robin said to her, "because it is a picture of someone special who captured my heart the moment I saw her, whom I know I will love in this life and into the next."

Celina trembled.

"I want you to look at her," he urged, "and realise why she means so very much to me."

Celina took a deep, painful breath. With the greatest difficulty she forced herself to look at the picture.

The next moment a gasp broke from her.

It was a picture of *herself*.

"I don't – understand – " she stammered.

Looking closely at the picture she could see that it had been produced recently.

"Who painted it?" she asked in wonder.

"My mother. She has been working on your portrait these last few days. She has always been a talented artist."

Light dawned on her.

"Is that why she has been studying me and giving me those intent looks?"

"That's right. She was making sure that she caught a good likeness. She knew exactly what I wanted."

"And what did you want?" she asked slowly.

"A portrait of the woman to whom I have given my heart. I wanted to give it to you. But before you accept it I want to tell you the story, so that you can understand why we are both here."

He took her hand and walked over to one of the tall windows, from where they could look out over his beautiful acres.

After a moment's silence he began,

"When I was very young I found it marvellous to go to the theatres in London and to meet those who sang and danced. They were a fascination I had never known and I went wild, indulging myself with every pleasure.

"Next I found France was even more exciting than England and there were even more women who were beautiful and exciting. I possessed a title and money and of course they drew me in, knowing that I would spend freely on them.

"None of them, I may tell you, lasted very long and it was years before I found one woman who seemed to fascinate me more than any of the others."

Celina felt now he had come to the most important part of his speech. She clenched her hands together until they hurt.

"She was beautiful and enticing and everywhere she went men rushed to her side."

He sighed.

And then he continued,

"I was proud and delighted that she favoured me and I gave her clothes and jewellery, some of which were family heirlooms. I wanted to be magnificent in her eyes.

"She was a professional dancer, but I thought everyone would come to accept her because she meant so much to me. I asked her to be my wife, not once but many times. But always there seemed to be a reason as to why she could not make up her mind to marry me."

He sighed again and there was silence for what seemed a long time.

"Finally I learnt the reason for all her delays and excuses. She had been married for nearly five years to a Frenchman who lived in the country and seldom came to Paris."

He drew breath before resuming,

"She went back to him sometimes and then returned to Paris, where she amused herself with me. I only found out the truth when Pierre Vallon became one of her admirers and stole from her the jewels I had given her. I had him arrested. He swore vengeance and the rest of the story you know.

"He was the thug who came the other night and tried

to kill you. If he had done so, I would have been completely to blame."

Celina could not speak and after a moment he went on,

"I had already become intrigued by you – the decisive way you acted over the tenants and the way you managed to keep me guessing as no other woman has ever been able to do.

"But it was only when I saw Vallon attack you that I finally understood the truth – that you mean more to me than words can say. You were fighting for me, my darling, and now I want you to know what you mean to me and how much I love you.

"If you had died, my own life would have been over. I only knew it in that moment, when it was almost too late. I know I am not worthy of you, but please believe me when I say that I can never love anyone in the same way that – I love you. I can only pray that your own feelings can somehow – because you are so good and generous – "

He broke off with an air of strain, as though this went too deep with him for mere words. She felt a tremor surge through him with the intensity of his emotion.

Suddenly he turned away and moved to open one of the windows, as if he needed the fresh air.

Then, as he stood almost with his back to Celina, she knew he was waiting for her to speak and that he was afraid of what she might say.

"Do you want me to say that I love you?" she asked.

"Only if it's true. I could not bear any pretence. If you do not love me, I will endure it and spend the rest of my life trying to win your love."

"Robin," she said softly, "my husband, I fell in love with you *years* ago."

"What?" He looked at her sharply.

153

She moved to stand before him.

"I knew I must not let you find out, so I played the part of a good friend, almost a sister, so that you should not suspect. All the time I longed for you to love me, but I knew I had no chance."

"Great Heavens! Why could I not see what was under my nose?"

"Because I didn't want you to."

He eyed her cautiously.

"I am getting a fearful suspicion that I have been dancing to your tune all this time."

"Would you mind?" she asked, smiling tenderly.

He shook his head and seized her in his arms, holding her close.

"As long as it's your tune, and nobody else's, my darling. I can see that you are going to rule my estate with an iron hand in a velvet glove. So why not me?"

"I cannot believe that this is happening to me," she murmured in a daze of joy. "I have loved you so much and longed to be your wife. When I was told you wanted me, I thought all my dreams had come true."

"But you turned me down," he pointed out, staring at her.

"Because of something I overheard you say. You told your mother that I was a countrified spinster who had been on the shelf for years. You even said I was inventing tales about receiving offers of marriage."

Robin groaned and struck himself on the forehead.

"You heard me say that? But where were you?"

"Just outside the door. I turned and fled straight home."

"Heavens what a dolt I was! How could you ever forgive me for such cruel, stupid words?"

"I thought I never could. And then you came to see me the next day just as Delaine appeared, and I was so glad that you could see for yourself that I was definitely not on the shelf."

"You really *did* turn down a Marquis for me," he ventured.

"How could I marry him when I loved you so much?" she answered tenderly.

"As I love you," he added quickly. "I love you with my heart and my soul. But I almost left it too late to see the truth."

"What truth?" she whispered. "Let me hear you say it."

"The truth that you are my heart and soul, my own true love forever. You are the woman I shall want always, the woman my heart has been waiting for all these years, although without knowing it."

She hardly dared to voice the next question and yet she knew she must.

"What about – the other woman?"

"She doesn't exist any more."

"Do you mean she is dead?"

"I don't know and I don't care. After the scandal I saw her no more. Probably she and her husband are in some other city deceiving other fools.

"Now I hate even her memory. She was evil and corrupt, while you are good and honest. I know that I can put my heart and my future into your lovely hands and that they will be safe forever.

"All I want is you, as I have never wanted any woman before. You speak to me with your heart and you saved my life. I am sure, my precious one, we can make our home a palace of happiness."

He took her in his arms in a fierce embrace. Celina surrendered herself to him, feeling his lips on hers and answering his passion with hers.

After a while he half released her, looking anxiously into her face.

"Can you truly love me now that you know the truth? I know I do not deserve your love. I deserve that you should leave me – except that I shall never let you."

"And I shall never leave you," she cried joyfully. "Never, never, *never*."

"You can really forgive me for everything?"

"There is nothing to forgive. Now that we have discovered our love, we can start the world anew. All I want is to be yours, to have your children and to be with you for the rest of our lives."

"For the rest of our lives," he repeated, smiling. "What beautiful words they are and what joy we will have making them come true.

"Come with me, my beloved, this room has nothing more to say to us. Together we have all the future ahead and it is time for our true marriage to begin."